Northern Light

Annette O'Hare

Dedication

Encourager: one who inspires with hope, courage, or confidence. Lovingly dedicated to those who have encouraged me on my journey and to my greatest encourager, Jesus Christ my Lord.

What People Are Saying

"From the first sentence to the book's stunning conclusion, Annette O'Hare's brilliant first novel *Northern Light* captured my heart. O'Hare's storytelling is flawless and her grasp of Texas history is spot-on. This tenth-generation Texan heartily approves! Do yourself a favor and savor this meeting of North and South on the Bolivar Peninsula. I promise it will be the best book you'll read in a very long time!"

~ Kathleen Y'Barbo, bestselling author

"North meets South in this romantic tale, filled with Texas-sized twists and turns. From a lighthouse on the Bolivar Peninsula to New York and then back again…this story will take you on a journey you won't soon forget. I'm happy to recommend this debut novel from author and friend, Annette O'Hare."

~ Janice Hanna Thompson, bestselling author

O send out Thy light and Thy truth: let them lead me; Let them bring me unto Thy holy hill, and to Thy tabernacles. ~Psalm 43:3

Part One

1

September 5, 1864, Bolivar Peninsula, Texas

"That smarts!"

Margaret Logan shucked the calfskin glove from her hand and stuck it under her arm. Pain coursed through her middle finger as blood pooled at the tip. A single crimson drop fell onto the prickly cotton boll that clung tightly to the bush.

Mama would have come up with a charming anecdote had she seen the deep red blood against the lily-white cotton. More than likely, it would have been some illustration concerning the blood of Jesus Christ and how it could wash a person white as snow.

Saving grace was the last thing on Margaret's mind. There was a long dingy sack trailing behind her that she needed to fill. Her family depended on the income they would receive come time to cash in their money crop: Sea Island cotton. She wiped the blood on the inside hem of her light blue apron and thrust her hand back inside the glove. The sight of blood sickened her. Plenty had been shed since the war began. Enough to fill a river from the Yankee North to the Confederate states of the South.

The war had taken everything that was good and decent and ripped it to shreds. She no longer knew the tranquility of her beautiful lighthouse home near New Orleans. Nor did she have the loving caress on her cheek of her beloved fiancé, Jeffrey Fontain. Instead, she wiped the sweat of hard labor from her brow with her own calloused hand.

"Margaret." Mama paused from her picking and raised her head. "The tide should be out by now. Go fetch your pail. We'll be needin' fresh oysters for the evening meal."

"Yes'm." She straightened. Pain surged through her back from being hunched over all afternoon pulling cotton. It made her happy to get out of the field for a while, even if it meant doing another chore.

Margaret's younger sister, Elizabeth, stood to her full height as soon as the words came from Mama's mouth. Her face pinched into a scowl and gloved hands flew to her hips. "Why can't I go too, Mama? Why does Margaret always get to go do the collecting?"

Mama pressed a palm against her back, a look of irritation etched on her face. "Because, Elizabeth, I happened to notice Margaret's sack is almost full and yours is lacking considerably. Besides, Margaret is the oldest, and I can trust her not to get distracted by every butterfly and black-eyed Susan she sees along the way. Now get yourself back to work and watch that sassy mouth of yours."

Elizabeth huffed and stamped her foot before

returning to her cotton pulling.

Margaret glanced at her mama, who gave her a nod and then turned away. She tugged the heavy cotton sack out of the field. It goaded Margaret to walk across the platform of what had been the base of the Bolivar Point lighthouse. Its absence had mocked her since the day they'd arrived on the desolate Bolivar Peninsula.

Not even Papa was cut out for the grueling work of pulling cotton. He was a trained light keeper, not a common farmer.

But like it or not, Margaret had to cross over the aggravating stretch of emptiness to hang her sack on the hook where they were stored. Removing her shoes, she collected her pail and slipped her feet into Papa's heavy boots. A mild September wind tossed her skirt around as if she were dancing a reel. Pink powder puffs grew wild in the sandy soil as she walked the path toward the bay. The delicate flowers swayed to and fro in the gentle breeze.

Margaret's feet slipped inside the oversized boots. The warm sun felt nice on her shoulders, not blazing hot as it had been only a month earlier. She sensed a slight whisper of change in the air as a song found its way into her thoughts.

"Oh! Lilly, sweet Lilly,
Dear Lilly Dale."

It surprised Margaret when the words escaped her lips. The sweet melody comforted her.

"Now the wild rose blossoms
O'er her little green grave."

The words caught in her throat, and she looked around, nervous that someone might be listening. Satisfied there was no one around for miles, she continued.

"'Neath the trees in the flow'ry vale."

The song sounded nice, even if the words spoke of a poor young girl's passing. Strange how death and dying didn't seem to bother her as they once did. The war-torn bodies of Confederate soldier boys they'd found floating at the water's edge cured her of any fears that death once conjured up.

A strong odor of fish emanated from the bay where she regularly collected oysters. The receded tide caused the foul smell, letting Margaret know it was the perfect time of day for gathering. She walked a good distance past where the water had been earlier.

Papa's heavy boots sank into the mushy sand with each step she took. It was a chore to pull her foot out without leaving the boot behind. She stepped over clumps of golden-colored seaweed amassed on the beach, left behind by the outgoing tide. A lone hermit crab picked up his shelly house and skittered for the water. Surprised by the sudden movement, Margaret stopped in her tracks, nearly falling over backwards.

Gathering food for the family was a welcome task. She would have rather rounded up a thick, juicy roast beef for their supper, but that was out of the question. Every head of cattle on the peninsula that the Confederate army hadn't procured had been pilfered by hungry Union raiding parties.

Her parents considered it a blessing to have access to the Gulf of Mexico and all the shrimp, crab, oysters, and fish they could eat.

But Margaret, her two younger sisters, and brother had grown tired of every kind of seafood the Gulf had to offer. Oh, how she missed the taste of beef. She smiled, secretly imagining running into a young man with a nice fat cow who would trade her for some magic beans. She chuckled.

The same gloves she'd used earlier in the cotton field were used to pick up the sharp oysters and place them in her pail. Back home, her mother had traveled the short distance to New Orleans to purchase seafood from the fish market. Now they depended on the land for their food, and if God didn't provide it, they didn't have it.

Mama would reason that if they didn't have it, they didn't need it.

Margaret would argue that point on a regular basis. There were several things she needed, like more books. But she'd all but given up on fighting that battle. *"The only book you need is the Good Book, and it's on the shelf."* Mama never listened to her. A girl stuck in the middle of nowhere, grieving the loss of everything she held dear, needed an escape, and she certainly wouldn't find that between the pages of the Bible.

Margaret came to a place where the pickings were abundant and filled her pail to the brim. One particular oyster caught her eye. She picked it up and noticed it stretched far beyond the end of her hand. *Oh, if only there was a pearl inside to match the size of the shell.*

The thought made her think of her family's yearly carriage ride to the Mardi Gras in New Orleans. How she missed the revelry, the mysterious, masked ladies in their magnificent flowing gowns. How they sparkled in the moonlight, their necks and ears dripping with diamonds and pearls. Beautiful, glistening pearls. Margaret swayed back and forth to a familiar melody, keeping time with the waves lapping around the big, cumbersome boots, the huge, sandy oyster clutched to her breast.

With a sigh, she dropped the shell onto the sand, as she'd already collected plenty for supper. She noticed something shiny hiding amongst the oysters. Bending over, she set her pail down and pushed away some of the rough shells to see what it could be. Without thinking, she picked up the artillery ball. Her cheeks heated, and she shot up from the ground, the shiny ordinance still in her hand. "Oh, Lord, can't I even do my chores without being reminded of the death constantly surrounding me?" she cried out in anguish and threw the ball down the beach. That's when she saw him.

The body lay half in, half out of the water. His clothing fluttered with the movement of the waves pulsing around him. Margaret looked heavenward and released a long breath. Slowly, she approached the bloody remains. His eyes were closed—he didn't move. She knelt beside him and gazed into his face. Her heart felt heavy. Had he left a young woman behind to grieve like her Jeffrey had? Did she even yet know of her loss?

Seawater colored the sailor's outer garment, making it look darker. The standard-issue gray wool kepi was missing from his head, his dark hair long enough to sway in the water. He wore a mustache and beard, the color a shade lighter than his hair.

Margaret extended a hand to his face. Such a handsome young man, probably the same age as her Jeffrey had been. She brushed sand from his cheek, her heart broken for whomever would grieve for him.

A long slash ran the length of his forehead, and there was a distinct hole in his shoulder. A bloody gash on his side all but cut his belt in half. Her hand stretched toward the tarnished gold buckle.

Realization dawned; the letters were not the Confederate *CS*, but the *US* of a Union sailor.

"Yankee!"

Her mind flashed through the stories she'd heard about Union men and the atrocities they'd performed against southerners…especially women. Yankee raiding parties had taken almost everything useful from the peninsula. Instinctively, she scanned the horizon in search of any approaching Union military men, sailors or soldiers. She had to get away before his fellow sailors returned to collect the body.

She crouched, poised to run.

Before she could withdraw her hand, his eyes shot open and he grabbed her wrist.

Margaret screamed in terror, trying to pull from his grip. What if he had a weapon? What did he plan to do to her? She pounded on his arm with her other hand, trying to free her wrist. But his grip was tight.

"Please help me." His voice was almost too weak to hear, but he peered straight into her eyes. His hand went limp and fell to the sand.

Margaret stood and backed away, but both boots stuck deep in the sand. She lost her balance and fell backwards, landed on something sharp. The sleeve of her dress ripped. She grabbed her arm as blood seeped through the tear. A bloody, jagged shell had mangled her wrist. Tears threatened, but terror held them at bay and gave her the clarity she needed to get away.

Margaret pushed off the sand and pulled her feet out, boots and all. Righting herself, she backed away, holding her injured arm, chest heaving with every breath.

Without a second thought about the pail containing the family's supper, she turned toward the trail, ready to bolt. But something tugged at her heart, urging her not to run…those pleading blue eyes. She moved a safe distance from the sailor. Her mind raced. *What do I do? Should I help him? Is he dead now? He did ask for my help—but he's a Yankee…*

"Papa will know what to do." She hiked up her skirt and took off. Despite the fact that her father's awkward boots sank in the sand with every footfall, she quickly reached the trail toward home.

Before the sailor was completely out of sight, Margaret glanced over her shoulder for another look at him, wondering if the ordeal had actually happened. But the searing pain shooting through her bloody arm gave her all the proof she needed.

The man seemed to be awake again and was feeling around for something.

Her hand covered her mouth and she let out a loud gasp. *Dear Father in heaven, he's looking for his gun!*

2

"Papa, Papa, come quick!" Margaret raced up the property line toward the house. Her frantic cries demanded the attention of the entire family.

The youngest two Logan children, four-year-old June and baby Jeremiah, peered through the window of the front room.

Papa emerged from behind the shed, a hammer held high as if ready for an attack. "What's going on out here?"

She needed to catch her breath.

Papa was the first to reach her side.

Mama and Elizabeth rushed out of the cotton field toward her.

"What on earth happened, Margaret?" Mama gave her a good looking over. "Did you fall? Your backside is covered with sand."

Papa lowered the hammer. "Give her a chance to speak, Caroline. She's plumb out of wind."

Elizabeth pointed at Margaret's torn dress and blood-stained arm. "Oh, my goodness, look at her arm, Mama. She's bleeding!"

Mama ripped the sleeve even further, revealing the long jagged cut left from the oyster shell. "That's a nasty gash, Margaret. Let's go in the house and get that taken care of." Mama tried leading her toward the house, but she didn't budge. "Now come on…"

"Mama…wait just a minute…please!" She pressed her injured arm to her chest. She cared not that blood from her arm seeped into the bodice of her dress, possibly ruining the garment. She pointed toward the bay with her other hand. "There's a man. I thought he was dead…but he wasn't."

Mama's eyes narrowed. "Did he hurt you? Did he do this to you?" She looked at Papa. "Jebediah, someone has hurt our girl."

The front door flew open and June ran out. Baby Jeremiah toddled as fast as his legs could carry him to Margaret's side.

The sight of blood had drawn them like flies to molasses.

"Sissy, what happened to you?" June asked.

Mama attempted to shoo them back into the house.

Papa looked squarely into Margaret's eyes. "Did he hurt you, Margaret?" He touched her trembling arm.

Margaret shook her head and waved her hand. "No, Papa, he didn't do this to me. I fell on a sharp oyster shell, and it cut my arm open." She struggled to get the words out. "He's…he's a sailor—and he's half dead."

Papa stepped closer, his voice steady and calm. "All right then, Margaret, tell me exactly what happened."

"He's a Yankee, Papa!"

Elizabeth and June clasped their hands over their mouths.

Baby Jeremiah slapped tiny hands over his face too.

Papa had given strict warnings to his daughters about steering clear of anyone who even remotely resembled a Union soldier.

"Whatcha gonna do, Papa?" June asked.

Mama slipped an arm around Margaret's waist and eased her head onto her shoulder. It calmed her nerves when Mama stroked her long hair.

Papa rubbed his stubbly jawline. "Well, I suppose we ought to go see what we can do." He turned to his youngest daughter. "June, go fetch my rifle and powder flask."

"You gonna shoot him, Papa?" June asked. The unexpected excitement seemed to have the little girl wound up.

Papa furrowed his eyebrows and shook his head. "No, June, I'm not planning to shoot anyone. I just want to be cautious and make sure everyone is safe, that's all."

"But you *might* shoot him, right, Papa?"

"All right now, run along and get the rifle and powder flask." Papa turned to Mama. "Caroline, go in the house and tend to Margaret's arm. While you're in there, gather some extra bandages. Sounds like we might need them." He handed the hammer to his middle daughter. "Put this away in the shed, Elizabeth. I also need you to haul in those cotton sacks from the field. I'm guessing we're done pulling for today. And when you get done with that, meet me out by the pen; I need a hand hitching the mule to the wagon."

~*~

Mama slung Jeremiah over her hip and helped Margaret into the house, even though she didn't really need help. The trip to the kitchen was made even more difficult with June helpfully pushing her from the rear. Mama and June eased her into a chair. She didn't squelch their doting; she didn't have the energy.

Mama set Jeremiah down and collected a bowl of water and a rag to clean Margaret's wound.

The little boy held out his arms for Margaret to pick him up. She instinctively pulled him onto her lap, forgetting the pain from the gash.

Little June's eyes grew at the sight of her baby brother climbing on her injured sister. Tiny hands gripped her hips. "Jer'miah, you get down off her right this instant!"

Jeremiah buried his face in Margaret's chest at June's scolding.

Mama pursed her lips. "Let him be, June. He's worried about Margaret, and it's time for his nap." Mama rummaged around in the cabinet where their meager medical supplies were kept. The roll of gauze was almost gone. Between the four kids and Papa, Mama had doctored more scrapes and cuts than should be allowed.

Mama took down the bottle of laudanum and slipped it into her apron pocket.

"The cut isn't that bad. I don't need the laudanum."

Mama dipped the rag into the water and then washed blood and sand from the jagged wound.

Margaret pressed her baby brother to her chest and winced at the pain.

"I know, Margaret. It's not for you. Now come with me into the bedroom so I can see what we have in the rag basket." Mama turned to June, who watched with great interest. "Young lady, your papa told you to do something. Now you'd better get to it."

"Oops…I forgot." June's eyes widened and she ran from the room.

Margaret followed Mama into the bedroom. She held tight to Jeremiah with her good arm and kept the injured arm close to her chest. Mama sat in front of the rag basket and Margaret sat on the floor beside her.

Jeremiah crawled out of her lap and laid his head on Mama's legs. He rubbed his eyes while chanting the name he called her, "Ma, Ma, Ma, Ma." Finally, he slept.

Mama firmly tied strips of a discarded pillowcase around her arm. When the wound was properly covered, she went to work tearing rags into bandages, handing some to Margaret too. It goaded her to think the precious strips of cloth would soon be used to doctor the Yankee sailor.

"So how bad did he look?" Mama's voice was soft as she glanced at Jeremiah.

Margaret squinted at the memory of what she'd seen. "He looked pretty bad to me, all bloody and shot up."

Little June came into the room and wiped her brow. "Whew, that rifle is mighty heavy." She brushed off her hands on her skirt. "Can I go see the Yankee, Mama?"

Mama tilted her head to look at her youngest daughter. "No, I need you to stay here with Jeremiah while I go with Papa and Margaret to see what we can do."

"But, Mama, I ain't never seen no Yankee before." The little girl whined and puffed out her bottom lip.

"Oh, my goodness, is that proper English, young lady?"

"No, ma'am."

"Now say it the right way."

Margaret turned away so June wouldn't see her smile.

June frowned and crossed her arms. "OK. I have never seen a Yankee before." Her arms dropped down to her sides as she jutted her chin out. "Mama, why am I the only one in this house who has to use proper English?"

"Every one of my children is taught proper English...it's up to them to use it. And thank you. That was much better," Mama said.

Margaret made eye contact with Mama, knowing she was probably fighting back a smile too.

June's eyes grew wide. "So can I go? I really want to see what he looks like, Mama!"

"Not this time. Stay here and keep an eye on Jeremiah until Elizabeth finishes her chores. Besides, you'll probably be seeing him before you know it."

Mama can't really be thinking about bringing him here! Margaret ripped the old sheet into strips. The ragged fabric would make fine bandages...*even if they might be used on that stinking Yankee.*

June plopped down beside her sleeping brother. "Dumb ol' baby."

Mama took a quilt from the bed and spread it over Jeremiah. "Now that will be enough of that, young lady, you hear me?"

"Yes, ma'am." June lay on the floor next to her brother.

"We'll send Elizabeth in directly. Come on, Margaret. If he's as bad as you say, then we better hurry."

Margaret helped gather the scraps of cloth and

then followed Mama outside.

~*~

Margaret watched Papa and Elizabeth attempt to attach the harness to the wagon. The mule brayed and kicked. It had been a while since the old girl had been hooked up to a harness, and she'd never liked it too much.

"Come on, Celia girl, you're going to ruin my wagon if you kick it too many more times." Papa talked to the animal as though she was another one of his daughters.

Margaret chuckled at the way her father dealt with the stubborn animal. "I think that's her intent, Papa."

Elizabeth held tight to the mule's harness. "Margaret, we really don't need any of your remarks right now!"

"Well, pardon me." The tension between Margaret and her sister grew with every passing day.

"All right, girls, that's enough of your bickering." Mama placed the supplies in the small cart.

Elizabeth released her hold on Celia. "Papa, I hauled in the cotton sacks, and I hung them on the hooks like you asked. So can I go to the bay with you?"

Margaret thought it a good idea. Anything to keep her from having to look at the horrible, bloody body of that Yankee would suit her just fine.

Papa was about to answer when Mama interceded. "No, I need you inside the house to watch over your sister and brother. Who knows how long we'll be gone."

Elizabeth's mouth drew up tight. "That's not fair, Mama! I did what Papa told me as fast as I could. Why does Margaret get to do everything, and I never get to do anything?"

Margaret gave her sister a warning look. It was never a good idea to argue with Mama.

Mama turned to Elizabeth. "And just what is it that Margaret gets to do that you don't? Collect oysters? Haul water for laundry? Because if it's more chores you want, I'll be more than happy to assign them to you. Is that what you want?"

Elizabeth hung her head. "No, ma'am."

"Mama, why don't you let Elizabeth go? I'll watch the little ones. Besides, I have no desire to take another look at that nasty, bloody Yankee." Margaret attempted to break the tension.

"Mama, can Margaret watch over June and Jeremiah instead of me?" Elizabeth looked at her. Tears coursed down her cheeks.

Mama took the bottle of laudanum and placed it atop the bundle of bandages already in the wagon. "No…Margaret is the one who knows where the man is, and she is the one who's going with us to the bay. Now, I told you what I need you to do. I suggest you get to it."

Elizabeth looked defeated. She turned to her father. "Papa?" Elizabeth whined and pleaded with outstretched arms, tears still flowing.

"Do what your mama says, Liz." Papa turned away and slapped Celia on the rump. "Come on, girl."

"We'll be back as soon as we can." Margaret spoke.

Elizabeth lifted her apron and scrubbed the tears from her face. She stomped into the house without another word.

Margaret ached for her rebellious sister.

Elizabeth's defiance had become a constant source

of pain. Twice in one day she'd complained of unfair treatment. Mama would probably give her a lesson on what was fair and what was not. Margaret turned to follow Mama and Papa. They were already halfway up the trail. Gathering her skirt, she hurried along to catch up with them. A chill ran down her spine at the thought that the man might have a gun. What would happen if they arrived to find a detachment of Union soldiers had arrived to collect their dead? Why couldn't Mama just leave well enough alone? Didn't their family have ample problems already without running to the rescue of a Yankee sailor? As far as Margaret was concerned, the Confederates had already decided this sailor's fate and it wasn't their business to meddle in their affairs.

The farther they went down the trail, the more Margaret wanted to run in the opposite direction. The image of the sailor's body caused bile to rise in her throat, but then, his smoky blue eyes found their way into her imagination. How she longed for him to still be alive so she might have the chance to see his beautiful eyes once again. She shook her head to remove the image and chastised herself for harboring such a thought about a Yankee.

3

Mama urged them to hurry and get to the sailor. Margaret would have rather stopped to enjoy the beautiful setting sun. But that wasn't going to happen. Just one more thing she could blame that Yankee for.

Papa led Celia through the tall grass until they reached the dunes. He pulled on the mule's harness. "Margaret, come up front so you can tell us which way to go."

She scanned the water's edge and noticed her pail shining in the setting sun. His body had to be nearby...she remembered dropping the pail. It didn't seem that he had been so far away when she found him earlier. It was no wonder she was so out of breath when she arrived back at the house.

She pointed out the direction to Papa, and he nudged the old mule forward, her bray indicating her opposition to the idea. "I'm sorry, girl; I know you don't like walking on the sand. Just a little further now." Her papa was sweet to everyone...even an ornery old mule.

The man was still half out of the water.

"Be careful, Mama. He grabbed my wrist." Margaret kept her distance. "And he might have a gun too."

Mama knelt by his side, inspecting his wounds. Margaret kept her distance after the scare he gave her earlier. At the frightful memory she crossed her arms tightly around her waist. Her wrist stung with her tight grip. "And remember…he might have a gun too."

Mama reared back and gasped as a fiddler crab ran across the sailor's torso.

Papa knelt in the sand on the other side of the body. He brushed the little crab off the man's chest with a chuckle and searched his clothing. "Don't worry. He's unarmed." Papa looked up at her. "He was probably sent ashore to look for food and this happened." Papa stood guard, rifle in hand.

Mama knew a lot about medicine because her papa, Grandpa Brannon, had been a doctor. She had even trained to become a nurse until she met Papa and everything changed…the first time she looked into Papa's eyes. She'd told the story often enough to her daughters.

"Is he alive?" Margaret asked.

Mama lowered her head to the man's face, and then looked at Papa. "He's still breathing, but not very strong. These wounds are pretty bad, Jeb. It's hard to tell how much blood he's lost with him being in the water. I'm not sure he'll make it." Mama looked at the man. "So young too."

Margaret found it difficult to care whether the man lived or died. What if this Yankee was the one who killed her Jeffrey? Why should her parents risk their lives and the lives of their children to help a blue belly? Sometimes her folks did things she couldn't for the life of her understand. And this was one of those times.

Papa lifted the man and dragged him out of the water.

"Be careful, Jeb. He's starting to come around."

From the agonizing groans, his pain must have been excruciating. She turned away, disgusted by the blood oozing from his wounds, mixing with the wet sand.

"Margaret, come give us a hand. I don't think me and Papa can lift him by ourselves."

She whipped her head around and glared at Mama. What could the woman possibly be thinking? "I'm not going to touch that filthy Yankee!"

"Margaret Frances Logan…get your hind end over here and help us load this young man into the wagon. If we don't get him back to the house, he has about as much chance as a candle in a windstorm of surviving."

Margaret felt the blood leave her face. "You're taking him to our home?"

"Well, what on earth did you think we would do with him?" Mama looked at Margaret as if she'd grown an extra head.

"I don't know, bandage him up…leave him here…take him to Fort Greene. But take him to our house? Please, Papa!"

Her papa stood but remained silent. He wasn't likely to take her side. *Meddling in the affairs of women isn't a pastime smart men partake in.*

She heard his all-too-familiar words in her mind.

"If we leave him here, he's sure to die. If we take him to the fort, they will probably put a bullet in his head," Mama said. "The Christian thing to do is take him home and patch him up."

Margaret's hands shook, she was so angry. She crossed her arms to steady herself. "So that's it…you care more about this dirty, rotten Yankee than you do your own flesh and blood?"

Mama stood, hands on her hips. "Margaret, why

did Jesus tell the story about the good Samaritan?"

"Mama, this isn't the time or the place to talk about Bible stories." Margaret raised her eyebrows and twisted her mouth to the side, satisfied she had the upper hand on her mama.

"Well, I think it's the perfect time, young lady."

Now both were standing face to face.

"You'd better answer your mama." Papa moved the rifle to the far side of the wagon and covered it with a cotton sack.

"I guess He told the story because He wanted us to know how we should treat people." Margaret huffed out her breath. Her shoulders sagged. Mama had won this round. "But that has nothing to do with us...a poor southern family helping a dirty...murderin'...Union sailor. Surely there are some things even God doesn't expect us to do. We can't all be Samaritans."

"The meaning is the same, dear. God wants all of His people to act like that Samaritan." She touched Margaret's arm. "What if we were from the North and it was Jeffrey laying there dying?" Mama's voice turned syrupy. "Wouldn't you want some godly person to help him?"

Margaret's bottom lip quivered. How could Mama stoop so low as to bring Jeffrey into the conversation? "That is a mean thing to say, Mama. My Jeffrey is dead and nobody was there to save him...nobody!" Tears began to flow.

"I know that, baby girl, but now we have the opportunity to do something right for one of God's creatures, in spite of this horrible war." Mama put her arms around Margaret and squeezed tight.

Mama's words hurt, but still, Margaret knew what her mama said was true. If the North and South would learn to get along, then this horrific war could be over sooner. Margaret joined her parents in lifting the Yankee into the wagon. As they maneuvered him on the buckboard, she averted her eyes. Mama was sure to stretch her sparse medical knowledge to its limit with this patient.

Mama crawled inside and went to work, tearing open his already shredded jacket to reveal his injuries. With the thick strips of cloth, she wrapped the flesh wounds on his broad forearms. Her hand disappeared in the man's overgrown, thick black hair. His eyes fluttered as she put the laudanum elixir to his mouth.

His face, the one Margaret had felt so compelled to touch only hours earlier, seemed pale against his dark facial hair. She turned away and scolded herself for having the gall to look on the face of that Yankee when her Jeffrey lay cold in his grave.

"Come on, Jeb, we need to get going before nightfall." Thankfully, Mama broke into Margaret's thoughts.

"Um-hmm." Papa nodded his head. "We don't want to be caught with a Union sailor come time for the foot patrols to start their evening rounds."

Margaret struggled to breathe when she heard her father's words...something she hadn't even considered. They could all be killed if the Rebels caught them giving aid to a Union sailor. Before she could utter her complaint, Mama looked straight at her.

"Gather up your pail and continue collecting oysters for supper. We still need to eat. You can catch up to us on the trail." Mama's matter-of-fact way of speaking suggested no questions were needed.

Margaret didn't voice the opinion that screamed

through her mind. *An extra mouth to feed!* She didn't deem it wise since Mama sounded so annoyed with her following their confrontation, but she was more than happy to finish the chore rather than accompany her parents back to the house...especially with that Yankee in tow.

Papa nudged Celia toward the trail. "Come on, girl. Let's get this boy back to the house before it's too late." The mule complied with a bit of coaxing.

Margaret gathered the spilled oysters. The huge shell that caught her attention previously found its way back into her hand. Thoughts of the Mardi Gras and home brought on an overwhelming sadness. She sank to her knees. Her skirt caught on Papa's boot and ripped off part of the bottom ruffle. The blood-stained frock was already destined for the rag basket, and there certainly weren't any ball gowns in her future. She might never be able to return to her beloved New Orleans.

The newspaper account of the fall of New Orleans reached them long ago. Papa figured Captain Farragut must have arrived shortly after they had left. The women of the family all cried as he read the news. Margaret stroked the rough shell and allowed her mind to wander—New Orleans, her beautiful pearl, was gone. Even if they could go home, would there be anything left? She threw the big oyster shell as far as she could.

Thoughts of the war brought her back to the current disaster...the one headed toward her home. She pushed up off the ground and thought about the calamity her mama and papa were bringing on their family.

She rubbed sandy palms on her filthy skirt and

finished filling the pail with oysters. Someone with common sense needed to be present when her parents arrived with the Union sailor. And if that was her…then so be it.

4

Thomas Murphy lifted his head and tried to focus. He was on a boat surrounded by a dense layer of fog. At least he thought it was a boat. Why else would he feel the waves and swells tossing around?

The image finally became clear...yes...there was a lighthouse in the distance. He could discern only the long golden beam stretching out across the water. The longer he gazed at the beacon, the clearer it became. Wait...he wasn't in a boat; it was a soft bed. The lighthouse was only a painting. The intense throbbing in his head was the source of the waves and swells. He dropped back onto the soft pillow.

He raised his hand to his forehead and felt a large bandage covering the warm, sensitive area. Pain in his shoulder forced his hand back down from his bandaged forehead. He rolled to his side and looked around the room. It didn't appear to be a hospital. He tried to remember what happened. *Think, Thomas, think. Where could ye be?*

Shadowy memories of burning hot ordinance, the smell of smoke, and a sense of falling swam through his mind. The room swirled, making him want to retch. He'd been in enemy territory. He reached under the sheet to check for his weapon but only felt the bare flesh of his thigh. Someone had stripped off his clothes and bandaged his wounds. Seething pain overcame him. The fog returned, and then the room grew dark.

~*~

Margaret slipped inside the front bedroom and inched toward the bed where the sailor slept.

Mama had kept him knocked out with laudanum because with all the thrashing about he did, she didn't want him busting open the stitches.

The even rise and fall of his ribcage told Margaret he was still alive. It was inappropriate for her to tarry alone in the room, but she had good reason. Anything that could be used as a weapon needed to be removed. She touched a lace doily and looked at the sailor. "No, I suppose you can't hurt us with a doily." She replaced the hand-crocheted decoration and then moved to the dressing table. There was a comb, a brush, a mirror...and a letter opener. "You won't be stabbing any of us with this, sir." She slid the thin sliver of silver inside the pocket of her apron.

Margaret scowled at the man, resenting how peaceful he looked asleep on some of their best sheets. She moved closer to the bed. "Well, Mr. Yankee sailor, I guess you think everything is going your way, don't you? Get yourself shot up and just happen to land in the home of some honest, God-fearing people who patch you up and let you recover in one of their bedrooms. Well, guess what?"

The sailor stirred and moaned.

Margaret froze. He waved his arm back and forth and mumbled something she couldn't understand. She had spoken too loudly.

He sighed and settled back into sleep.

She released the breath she'd been holding and clutched her chest, willing her heart to stop pounding.

She took one last quick survey of the room, put her hand against the letter opener in her apron pocket, and headed for the door.

The last thing she wanted was for her face to be the first thing the sailor saw when he finally opened his eyes.

But feeling as guilty as Lot's wife, she glanced back at the bed for one more look.

~*~

"Would you like some tea, Thomas?"

The dark-haired beauty stood beside his bed, ready to tend to his every need. "Why, thank ye, lass. That would be wonderful."

She leaned close and stroked his cheek, genuine concern shining in her eyes. "You poor thing, you're badly injured. Why would anyone want to hurt you?"

Thomas reached for her hand, but now she was holding a tray of tea and biscuits. "Aye, lass, but that's how it goes in war, I suppose."

She seemed to float to his bedside. She smelled of roses and fresh country air.

"The angels must be smiling on me today. I don't know what I've done to deserve having such a gorgeous woman by my side."

The beautiful apparition with the coal-colored hair floated toward the door without serving him tea. The door creaked when she opened it.

As Thomas woke, pain covered him like a blanket...it had all been a dream.

~*~

Someone watched him from the crack in the door.

Thomas tried to focus, but the stupor he was in made it difficult. He tensed, searching for a weapon. The tiny round face only reached up to the doorknob, so whoever was looking at him must not be very old. "Hello there, wee one." His voice sounded hoarse and raspy. He cleared his throat.

The eyes doubled in size and the door slammed shut.

"Mama, Mama, the Yankee is alive!" A little girl's voice rose outside the room. "And he talks funny too!"

Thomas chuckled, which sent a surge of pain through his torso. He sobered. There was no denying who he was to those who had apparently saved his life.

As he lay in the darkened bedroom, footsteps approached the room.

He covered what he could of his body with the soft, clean bed sheets.

The door swung open, and a woman stepped through holding a tray. Her face was gaunt, causing her cheekbones to protrude in much the same way his own mam's had. Even her arms looked slender but muscular. Bright red hair sprinkled with strands of silver was pulled into a knot at the nape of her neck. She appeared to have been a strong, hearty woman at one time. But the war had probably done its part to beat her down, as it had with everyone else. She didn't look dangerous. "Well, I see you've decided to join the living, Van Winkle. My name is Caroline Logan...and what is your name?"

"Thomas, ma'am, T-Thomas Murphy." He pulled the quilt up to his neck, despite the action causing him a great amount of pain.

"You needn't be afraid, Mr. Murphy. We don't

intend to hurt you."

"But ye must know I'm a Union sailor, ma'am. Yer young girl seemed to know." Thomas remained on guard, despite the fact he had nothing with which to defend himself.

"My, but you do have quite the accent." Caroline Logan smiled and moved faher into the room. She placed the tray of food on a chest at the foot of the bed and stood with her hands on her hips. "Where exactly is it that you are from, Mr. Murphy?"

Thomas tried to clear his throat but decided against it as the pain was unbearable. "Originally from Ireland, ma'am, but I suppose now I'm from New York."

A tiny pair of eyes once again appeared beside the doorjamb. Another small face appeared below the first one—this one looked even younger.

"We have company, ma'am."

Mrs. Logan whipped around toward the door. "June, Jeremiah, you may come in now. They've been chompin' at the bit to meet you since we brought you here."

Thomas was set at ease by the angelic faces of the little girl and boy. He pondered how their chubby-cheeked smiles could seem so normal and happy when the country they lived in was being torn apart by war.

Mrs. Logan gathered the children to her. "Mr. Thomas Murphy, this is June and Jeremiah Logan, my two youngest children."

"Pleased to meet you, Mr. Murphy." The little girl extended her tiny hand.

Thomas leaned forward to accept it. A terrific pain shot through his side. He emitted a low, guttural cry as he grasped for the area.

Jeremiah's eyes grew wide with fear, and the child fled from the room crying.

June drew back her hand and buried her face in her mama's skirt.

"Oh, I'm so sorry to have frightened yer wee boy, ma'am. I seem to have found a new source of pain." Thomas fell back. He clutched at his bandaged side and slowly breathed in and out, willing the pain to go away.

"That's quite all right, Thomas. I suspect you're feeling your stitches. I sewed up a mighty big gash on your side there. Oh, and I also dug a slug out of your shoulder. It's a good thing it wasn't an artillery ball or else you might have lost the arm. You're blessed that I had a full bottle of laudanum on hand."

"Are ye a doctor, Mrs. Logan?"

"No...but my father was. And I've had quite a bit of nursing training."

"So, ye been plying me with opium, have ye? And how long have I been here, ma'am?" Thomas lifted up again and then pulled on his beard growth to determine how long he'd been incapacitated.

Mrs. Logan removed her daughter from within the folds of her skirt, and the little girl left the room.

Caroline picked up another pillow and stuffed it behind Thomas's back. "You've been here three days, Mr. Murphy. And you should be glad I had that medicine." She wiped her hands on her apron. "Heavens...it took most of the family just to hold you down while I patched up your wounds." The woman sounded somewhat vexed. "It would have been nice if I had access to those mineral springs we passed back in the town of High Island when we moved out here. You'd be fit as a fiddle if you could soak your body in those hot springs. But I did the best I could with what I had."

"And indeed, I am thankful to ye, ma'am. I'm supposing I wouldn't be alive now without ye." He relaxed against the plush pillows, comfortable in the thought she mustn't want him dead since she'd gone to such lengths to keep him alive. "Ma'am, if ye don't mind me askin', will ye tell me why ye decided to save me life? I am the enemy, after all."

Mrs. Logan paused from puttering around the room. She appeared to be deep in thought. "Well, Mr. Murphy, I suppose it was the Christian thing to do. What kind of people would we be if we just left you there to die?"

"Now yer sounding like my mam." Thomas smiled at her.

"Ah, is she living back in New York?"

"No, ma'am, she's dead."

"Oh, I'm so sorry, Mr. Murphy."

"Don't ye worry about it none. She's been gone for some time now." Thomas paused and felt himself being pulled into the painting on the wall—effects of the opium, he suspected. The painful thought of his mother's death was one of dozens of memories he'd just as well forget. He turned his attention back to the woman and changed the subject directly. "And is there a Mr. Logan about?"

"Yes, there is. My husband, Jebediah, is working in the field picking cotton."

"Cotton, eh? And do ye gin it yerself, ma'am?"

"No, there's no gin on the peninsula that I know of, but we do use a bit of it here. You're resting your back on some right now."

"Very nice indeed. And what do ye do with the

rest of it? After all, the Union navy has most of this area under tight blockade." His own weakly spoken words brought back a fleeting memory of what he'd been doing before he was shot.

Caroline picked up the tray. "That's true, but we still have our ways of getting it to the mainland." She gingerly placed the tray on his lap. "The cotton is taken to the state penitentiary up in Huntsville for processing." She paused a moment. "Since you're awake, you might want to try eating something. Some folks around here have expressed they are mighty tired of feeding you."

"I understand and can't say that I blame them." Thomas picked up the spoon.

Caroline started for the door.

"Excuse me, ma'am, but would ye mind telling me if there are others who live here? I seem to have recollection of a dark-haired young woman floating around in my mind." Thomas stuck the spoon into the bowl and stirred it. "Aye, perhaps it was an angel I seen." He began to laugh, but a streak of pain shot all the way from the slash in his side to the deep hole in his shoulder. Thomas cried out in pain and grabbed the blanket, almost overturning the food on his lap.

Caroline rushed over to steady him. "N-now don't you start laughing or else you might bust open your stitches." Her hands and her voice trembled. "Try to eat some soup and cornbread and keep quiet." The woman gave a small smile. "You must be having memories of my eldest daughter, Margaret. She's the one who found you half-dead on the beach. Would you like to meet the two older children?"

"Indeed I would, ma'am. I'd like to thank Miss Margaret." Thomas lifted a spoonful of the steaming broth. The warm liquid soothed as it went down. He took a few more spoonfuls before his head fell to the side. Fog enveloped his brain as he relaxed against the pillows.

Caroline moved toward the door. "Margaret, Elizabeth, would you please come to the front bedroom?"

Her loud words jarred Thomas back to consciousness.

"I believe they are out in the kitchen fixin' up a batch of cookies to go along with the evening meal tonight." She wiped her hands on her apron. "They better not burn them. We're down to the last of the sugar and there's no more to be found."

"Aye, but I shall be a lucky man if yer daughters can cook half as good as ye have prepared this soup, Mrs. Logan."

"I didn't cook the soup...my daughter Margaret did." After a moment, Caroline called for the girls again. "Margaret, Elizabeth, come now, please."

The two girls scurried into the front bedroom.

"Mr. Murphy, these are my two eldest daughters, Margaret and Elizabeth. Girls, this is Mr. Thomas Murphy."

The younger of the two had brownish hair tied up in bows like a schoolgirl. Her yellow dress fit snug around her girlish, plump frame. She swayed as she stood with her hands clasped behind her skirt. Her face was dusted with flour, and her cheeks seemed to glow in the dimly lit room as she smiled.

He smiled back at her.

The other one stood silent. She didn't look at Thomas, then her sister elbowed her in the side, and a hint of anger etched her face. Eyes the color of violets met his own. His mouth became dry and he groped for the glass of water on the tray. He attempted to speak. "I'm...I'm pleased to meet ye, ladies. What a coincidence—I had a sister named Elizabeth too." He managed to get the words out before wiping his face with the napkin.

The younger girl curtsied, lifting her skirt out at the sides. "It's a pleasure to meet you too, Mr. Murphy."

The older girl narrowed her gaze at her sister and rolled those violet eyes before turning her glare toward Thomas. She folded her arms and stood, silent.

Her mother nudged her crossed arms. "Margaret."

The young woman dropped her arms, let out a huge sigh, and dipped her head. "Mr. Murphy."

Thomas needed to catch his breath. The girl was beautiful with the coal-colored hair of his dreams. Her skin looked soft as satin and smooth as porcelain china. "Miss Margaret, I understand yer the one who came to my rescue. I'm much obliged to ye, ma'am."

"You're welcome, Mr. Murphy. I hope you understand that I don't make it a general rule to go saving the lives of blue-bellied Yankee sailors, but according to my mama and papa, it was the right thing to do. Now if you don't mind, I have cookies to bake. Good day, sir." The words were spoken in a lovely, melodious voice. His stunning savior whirled around, her skirt flaring wide at the bottom as she rushed from the room.

Her mother and younger sister gasped in unified disbelief.

"I am so sorry about Margaret's rudeness," Mrs. Logan apologized.

Mother and daughter abruptly left the room. Mrs.

Logan was obviously angry.

The gorgeous young lady's words were definitely some of the harshest Thomas had ever heard, and yet he longed to hear her beautiful voice speak them once again.

5

Margaret slammed a huge ball of dough onto the kitchen counter and a cloud of flour exploded from beneath it. *Thomas Murphy…so that's his name.* She picked up Mama's rolling pin and hammered the crushed ball before rolling it flat as a piece of paper. *Mr. Murphy, shall I go fetch the authorities so it will be easier for you to turn us all in for treason?*

Little June pushed one of the kitchen chairs to the counter, climbed up, and watched her big sister. "Can I throw the dough ball, Margaret? I wanna make flour go everywhere too!"

"No! Now get down from that chair before you fall and hurt yourself." Margaret scraped up the flattened-out dough and rolled it back into a ball. She grabbed a handful of flour and threw it onto the counter in a huge white puff.

"Do it again, sissy! Make the flour go way up in the air!" June waved her hands above her head.

Heavy footsteps came up behind Margaret. Mama and Elizabeth would be hot on her heels…primed for an ambush. She pelted the counter with the ball of dough again.

Her little sister clapped her hands together and squealed with glee.

Mama stepped up behind June and lifted her out of the chair. She pulled it back to the kitchen table and patted her on the behind. "June, go to the front room with your brother."

"But, Mama, I wanna see sissy make more flour clouds."

"You heard me, now go!"

June poked out her bottom lip, crossed her arms, and stomped out of the room.

Margaret cast an uncaring but cautionary glance to her other side.

Elizabeth stood with hands on her hips, an imposing look on her face. She tapped her foot as though she had some kind of power over Margaret.

Margaret glared and the haughty look melted from Elizabeth's face.

Mama twirled Margaret around and pointed a finger squarely in her face.

Margaret grabbed hold of the counter she was backed up against. Childlike fear welled up inside.

"Margaret Frances Logan, I don't ever want to hear you talk to a guest in our home like that again, no matter who they are. Do you understand me?"

Papa chose that very instant to come through the back door. He took one look at the situation, shook his head, and headed straight for his chair and the newspaper he'd read at least a half-dozen times.

Mama made eye contact with Papa and then removed her finger from Margaret's face. She backed away and released a long, huffy breath.

Margaret placed her hands on her hips. "He's not a guest, Mama! He's a rotten, stinkin' blue-bellied Yankee who doesn't belong in our home!"

"What on earth is wrong with you, Margaret?" Elizabeth approached Margaret, gesturing toward the front bedroom. "Don't you even realize the most handsome man on the entire peninsula is right here in our house?"

Margaret and Mama jerked their heads toward Elizabeth.

A rosy glow crept onto Elizabeth's cheeks as her hands covered her mouth. Her eyes widened.

June came back into the kitchen.

Margaret hardly noticed her entrance.

A low groan came, and the sound of the newspaper being thrown to the floor came from the parlor before the front screen door creaked open and then slammed shut.

Mama was the first to break the silence. "Elizabeth Fay, you shouldn't be noticing men at your age. You're not even old enough to court."

June placed her hands on her hips, matching her mother's stance. "But, Mama...I heard Lizbeth say that Yankee's the only available man on the peninsula over the age of ten, besides Old Man Goodman." June cocked her head. "And if you ask me, Old Man Goodman is ugly as a mud fence and older than the dirt they built it with."

The tension instantly melted from Margaret's shoulders. She put one hand over her mouth while the other steadied her belly to keep from laughing out loud at her little sister's illuminating outburst.

Mama turned her back so the girls couldn't see her face. There was a slight bounce of Mama's shoulders before she grabbed hold of the counter and picked up a potholder to fan herself.

The look of horror on Elizabeth's face revealed how June's statement affected her.

Mama seemed to be searching for the right words to say.

Tears began to flow down Elizabeth's cheeks. She ran from the kitchen. A few seconds later, the bedroom door slammed.

Mama's eyes were dancing with laughter.

Margaret began to laugh and fell into Mama's arms. Margaret pulled her baby sister into their embrace and hugged her tightly.

June had a bewildered look on her face. She looked up at Mama and Margaret and shrugged her shoulders. "Mama, sissy, why did Lizbeth run off...and what in the world are y'all laughing at anyway?"

~*~

Margaret sat on the top stair in front of the house. A graceful roseate spoonbill swooped down, diving into the drainage pond that ran along the property line. A cool coastal breeze danced through acres of purple lovegrass. Gusts of wind rushed through the wheatgrass like waves crashing on the beach.

Elizabeth was still crying in the bedroom.

Her parents had put their family in danger by harboring the Union sailor in their home. Margaret slammed her fist against the wooden stair rail and grabbed her hand, wincing in pain. *Why am I acting like this? I've never had a temper. That stranger has me all tied up in knots!* She rubbed the side of her hand, feeling remorseful over her outburst. She should go to her sister and comfort her, but she was so upset with everyone in her family that Elizabeth would have to cry it out.

Her Jeffrey had always been clean-cut and clean-shaven. His hair would never have behaved like

Thomas's—so wavy and dark...framing his handsome...

She buried her face in her hands and tried to cry, but the tears wouldn't come. How could her sister possibly think that Yankee was handsome? Thomas's long hair was overdue for a trim. He looked like a vagabond in his tattered uniform with unkempt facial hair, and those eyes...those steel-blue eyes.

Margaret grasped her head in her hands. *What's wrong with me? Do I so desperately miss the love of a man that I would consider the likes of that Yankee?* "Oh, Lord, why did you have to take my Jeffrey away from me and only months before we were to marry?" She didn't bother wiping the tears away. She'd lost the love of her life, her home, and everything that was familiar. The war took nothing and no one into consideration. Young, old, man, woman, or beast, everyone suffered equally. Even the trip from Louisiana was a grueling ordeal that left its mark on the whole family—the checkpoints, the beggars, the gunfire, and the bodies...so many bodies of dead soldier boys.

And Mama, her belly about to burst with the twins. Margaret thought it cruel and merciless for God to make Mama carry a dead baby in her womb all the way across Louisiana. But it did seem the standard of the day they lived in. There was no fairness anymore—not for anyone.

She and her younger sisters had seen more death and unrighteous acts than young women should ever be exposed to. The smell coming from nearby Fort Greene wasn't only human waste, as she'd thought when she'd accompanied Mama to the fort to treat the injured following a raid. The smell was an accumulation of rotting septic wounds and all stages of death and dying that lingered amongst the prisoners. The putrid odor would live on in her mind forever.

Vermin and disease inhabited the place. Perhaps it was a good thing they didn't take Thomas there. A sickening feeling roiled in her stomach for even thinking it. She'd heard Papa say a soldier didn't have a snowball's chance in Hades of surviving Fort Greene, with the spread of dysentery and all, especially not a wounded soldier.

Why did there even have to be a war? Nothing was worth the loss of life and heartache the South had seen. Papa said the war started because of northern states wielding their powerful influence over the South. They took away the southern states' rights, including the owning of slaves to do all the hard work. There couldn't have been more than five people on the whole peninsula who owned slaves. Not counting the ones the Confederates used at the fort, of course. But her family had never owned any slaves and still they had to suffer the consequences of the war.

She'd never heard about local slaves being abused. But then again, why would anyone brag about such a thing? Margaret had met the Stoltzes' servant girl, Necie, a time or two. Was there a possibility Necie was unhappy? Had she been abused? Truthfully, Margaret had never thought about it. A sinking feeling overcame her heart at the realization that she'd never even cared.

A strong gust of wind blew into her face; the breeze whipped her hair. Slaves, war, states' rights— no young woman should have to think of such things. She should be taking care of her husband and awaiting the birth of their first child. But it wasn't meant to be.

Her mind drifted to the man convalescing in her family's guest bedroom. She banged her fists to her forehead to remove the thought. It was impossible though, as his long dark hair and unshaven chin seemed etched in her mind. "God, why did You have to send a Yankee? You know I need a man to love, and You send me a Yankee." She sobbed aloud. "And did You have to send the most handsome Yankee I've ever seen, Lord?"

"Margaret!" Mama called.

"Yes, ma'am!" she hollered back, scrubbing the tears from her cheeks with her apron. "I'm out front."

"Come clean up the mess you made in the kitchen, young lady! I can't believe you would waste so much good flour having your little tantrum. You know there's a good chance we won't get any more!"

Margaret brushed away sand that had collected on her skirt. She vowed never to think about Thomas Murphy in that way again.

The only problem…she had serious doubts she was strong enough to do it. "Coming, Mama!"

6

Thomas set the food tray on the dresser next to the bed. He would have taken the dishes to the kitchen, but Mrs. Logan refused to allow him to do anything. Even after two weeks of recovery, she insisted on him being waited on, much to the chagrin of all but one of the female children in the family.

Thomas had learned much about the close-knit family. The baby boy, Jeremiah, was everyone's pride and joy with his raven-colored curls and apple-red cheeks. He would probably be forever treated like a prince. The youngest girl, June, was the funny one. He would never forget their first real conversation without adult supervision.

"Mr. Murphy," June had said. "My big sister Margaret keeps callin' you a blue-bellied Yankee." She twirled a curl of the bright red hair she'd inherited from her mama. "Well, I was just wonderin' whether or not you really do have a blue belly." Her inquisitive innocence was refreshing.

Thomas chuckled. Elizabeth was a mystery to him. He knew the young thing harbored feelings that he'd politely rejected so as not to hurt the poor girl. She was barely in her teens.

The last time they'd spoken was particularly strange.

"Mr. Murphy." Elizabeth came into the bedroom.

She was hiding something and shut the door. She uncovered a plate of biscuits and a small pot of honey. "Here you go." She held the plate out to Thomas. "Mama was saving these for tomorrow, so don't tell anyone I gave them to you. It will be our little secret."

Thomas couldn't accept the gift. "Elizabeth, I don't think ye should take things without asking permission."

She scowled and continued holding the plate out to him. "But I took them for you!"

Thomas didn't know what to do.

After an awkward silence, Elizabeth slammed the plate onto the chest of drawers and stormed out of the room. There had been other disturbing conversations and situations. It seemed as though she wanted him to feel sorry for her in order to win his affections.

Margaret was the apple of his eye. The most beautiful thing he'd seen since leaving his homeland of Ireland. He couldn't stop thinking of the girl with the coal-colored hair, skin as smooth as fresh-churned butter, and those violet eyes. But she seemed to hate everything about him. He was the enemy.

The Logan parents, however, went out of their way to make him feel welcome.

Thomas patted his belly. He'd eaten more food since his injury than his whole time in the Navy. *Aye, but yer getting fat, Thomas Murphy.* He'd decided to get up and move around over the next few days in order to build up his strength. He was determined to somehow work for these fine people—to repay their kindness.

A tapping came at the door.

"Yes, come in."

Jebediah Logan entered the room, a smoldering pipe in his hand. He took a long draw from the beautifully carved wooden instrument before speaking. "Good afternoon, Mr. Murphy." Jebediah pulled up a chair and sat down.

"And a good afternoon to ye, Mr. Logan. How are things going with the cotton pulling?"

Jebediah released the smoke he'd inhaled, the slow stream escaping from his mouth. Mr. Logan did everything slow and easy. "Oh, we're just about done with the pulling. Now we gotta get it ready to take over to the docks for shipping. I've got Elizabeth and Margaret to help me with that though. Mostly, I've been working on the garden. About time to put out the winter vegetables." Mr. Logan wiped a bit of ash from his pant leg. "Well, son, you're looking a might better than when we first brought you here in the donkey cart. Are you feeling any stronger?"

"Aye." Thomas lifted his arm and made a muscle. "A wee bit every day."

An uncomfortable silence filled the room. Jebediah Logan was a man of few words.

It was up to Thomas to fill the void. "Mr. Logan, ye mind me asking a question on…a personal level?" Thomas averted his eyes and rubbed his leg.

"I suppose you're welcome to ask. But I'm not agreeing to answer until I hear what you have to say." Jebediah crossed his arms.

"Of course, sir. Y'see, I've been wondering since ye brought me here why yer not fighting with the Rebels."

"Oh, that…of course." Mr. Logan set his pipe on the tray and rolled up the right sleeve of his pale blue cotton shirt. "There was an accident at the lighthouse I manned down in South Louisiana."

"Oh my, sir, what on earth happened to yer arm?"

Thomas cringed.

"There was a strong, gale-force wind blowing that day, and I was having a hard time keeping the light lit. Anyway, I needed to fetch more oil, so I started down the stairs, which happened to be slick with seawater. Well, there weren't any handrails and my legs went out from under me. Just about that time, I heard a gust of wind come up, so I grabbed hold of the stair rung with all my might." Mr. Logan picked up his pipe and pointed it at Thomas. "It was either that or be thrown down the stairs and not be here today to tell about it."

Thomas waited for the man to go on.

"The wind that night was so strong it managed to pick my whole body up and flop it around like a sheet hung out to dry. My arm was pinned, and I couldn't let go. When the wind finally settled, I released my arm and crawled the rest of the way down the stairs. I felt the pain and then saw that the skin on my arm was shredded and the bones were broken to pieces." Mr. Logan rolled his elbow all the way around to the inside of his arm. "Caroline patched me up as best she could, but it's never been the same. It didn't help matters that I couldn't give my arm any time to heal. A lighthouse keeper has to keep things working or the results could be deadly."

"I can understand that, sir. So ye mustn't be very good with a gun then."

"No...I can shoot with my left but probably couldn't hit the broad side of a barn."

The two men laughed.

Mr. Logan rolled down his sleeve and buttoned it. "So, Mr. Murphy, Caroline tells me you're from Ireland."

"Yes, sir, that's right. My people come from

County Cork, the southernmost part of Ireland. It's a beautiful place, to be sure."

"Um-hmm." Mr. Logan put the pipe between his teeth, lit a match, and put it to the tobacco. He drew in four quick, hard puffs until smoke began to rise from the bowl. "So what brought you to America…fame, riches?"

"Aye, not so much fame as riches, I suppose. It was An Gorta Mór that brought us here. Ye know about the Great Hunger, don't ye?"

"I read about the potato famine in the papers. It was a terrible thing." A long, thick stream of smoke floated from his mouth.

"Aye, a most terrible thing, to be sure." Thomas bowed his head at the painful memory.

"Do you still have family back home, Mr. Murphy?"

"Call me Thomas, if ye please, sir. And no, I came here with my father and two brothers."

"All right then, Thomas, what about your mama— she didn't come to America with your family?"

"No, sir, she sacrificed her life saving her children from starvation. She wasn't the first to go though. My baby sister, Elizabeth, passed before Mam. She was a precious little thing with her curly auburn hair—it was the fever that took her from us." Thomas steeled himself as tears threatened in a wave of grief.

Mr. Logan lowered his pipe. "I'm sorry to hear that. Sounds as if you've had about as tough a life as any."

"I don't know, Mr. Logan. I've heard stories since I joined the Navy that make mine seem weak. Families from both sides have lost all their sons to the war."

"What about your brothers—did they join the

Navy with you?" Mr. Logan leaned back in his chair.

"Aye, my brother Jonathan joined with me, but the youngest, Michael, volunteered to work at DeCamp General Hospital on David's Island in New York so he'd be close to my pap in the town of Yonkers. Jonathan was put on a gunboat, and I was assigned to a blockade ship." Thomas looked toward the window and dragged his fingers through his thick, overgrown hair. He released a long breath. "Alas, I haven't been in contact with any of them for a ver' long time. I miss them somethin' awful."

Mr. Logan rubbed his jaw, gazing out the window, and then turned back to Thomas "So, what are your views on the war?"

The hair bristled at the back of Thomas's neck as an uncomfortable tightness crept up his spine. He wouldn't lie about how he felt. "Well, Mr. Logan, I think this war is a terrible thing. I see no good in pitting brother against brother because the North and South cannot come to an agreement. But I also think slavery is a horrible institution, and if it takes war to put an end to it...then so be it." Thomas prepared himself to be thrown out of the house. But instead of the rage he expected, Mr. Logan took a puff from his pipe and grinned—which somehow frightened him even more.

"Coming from Ireland, you must know what it's like to be a slave then."

"What?"

"I understand the Irish are the barely paid slaves of the North. Am I correct?"

"Well, I suppose ye could say that." Thomas scratched his head. "I can attest to the fact that it were the Irish who dug the canals, and it were the Irish who laid the railroads up north, and for what…a penny and a pat on the back. That's what! And me people are no more welcome to associate with the hoity-toity New Yorkers than the Negro is with his owner." Thomas braced his side. The outburst caused a sudden ache to arise. *How did he do that? I was quite prepared to defend the North and the man causes me to curse the very town I come from.*

Mr. Logan raised a single eyebrow and his mouth curled up in satisfaction. "Sorry, Mr. Murphy, didn't mean to rile you so. Do you want to know my opinion?" He held the bowl of his pipe and pointed at Thomas with the mouthpiece. "This war did not start out to be about slavery as you may believe. Of course, there are plantation owners willing to send their sons to their death to keep their slaves. But did you know that the tyrannous North refuses to recognize the rights of the South?" Mr. Logan's voice got higher and louder with each word. "Did you know the South is only allowed to sell its cotton and raw materials to northern factories? We can't sell out of the country either. And worse yet, the North has the backing of Congress, who levies the taxes so high on their finished products that we can't even afford them down here. And that, my friend, is why the South made the decision to secede from the Union."

Thomas squirmed a bit in the bed. Anything he said could be taken the wrong way, and he in no way wanted to offend the man who was feeding him. He changed the subject. "So, Mr. Logan, what are ye planning to plant in yer garden?"

Mr. Logan relaxed back in his chair and took a draw from his pipe. "I've got a good batch of seeds saved up from last year's crop. We'll be putting out turnips, lettuce, Brussels sprouts, collards, spinach." A grin rose on the man's face. "And here's one you'll like…Irish potatoes!"

Thomas laughed. The thought of digging his hands into soil gave him a good feeling. "Mr. Logan, do ye think I might be able to help ye with yer garden, sir?"

"Well, I don't know. Seems the missus has you on a pretty short leash. I'll have to check with her whether or not you're able to leave the house yet. But that would sure free me up to do some other things around here."

"Oh, I'd be much obliged if ye would ask. I'm so ready to get out of this bed."

Mr. Logan laughed. "I'll have Margaret prepare the seeds, and I'll see what I can do to get you a reprieve from the warden. Oh, but if you do get Caroline to give you a work permit, take care that you steer clear of my beehives. I don't want you swoll up with bee stings."

"Aye, so ye keep bees. Do ye get much honey from yer hives?"

"We get a fair amount of return. Enough to slather on our biscuits and sweeten our coffee, I suppose." He nodded his head. "Oh, and we use the wax for our candles too."

Thomas was excited at the thought of getting on his feet again. "Mr. Logan, do ye mind if I ask ye another question, sir?"

"I supposed there's not much I can do to stop you."

Thomas was growing to like this man. "Well, I was wondering…you and yer wife have treated me with such hospitality. And yer children have all taken to me—all...except for...one, yer precious Margaret. I don't understand why the young woman feels so much hatred toward me. She's such a beautiful lass...I hate for her to harbor such awful feelings inside. It can't be good for her."

Mr. Logan puffed on his pipe and gazed up at the ceiling as if thinking how to answer the question. "Thomas, my daughter has seen a great many disturbing things since this ol' war began. It broke her heart when she found out I was being recommissioned out here by the Confederate States Lighthouse Bureau.

"Then we arrived to find that the light had been dismantled for its iron. You see...New Orleans had always been her home, and she loved it dearly. She was devastated when we learned it had fallen to the enemy." Mr. Logan leaned forward in the chair. "You probably don't know it, but back in Louisiana she was engaged to be married. Her fiancé was killed about a month before her wedding day. They had to postpone the date at least a dozen times, but their day never came."

The man's words pierced Thomas's heart. It all made sense now. "I'm so sorry to hear that, Mr. Logan. The poor lass..."

Jebediah lowered his pipe, the tobacco smoked to ashes. "Well, I suppose I'd better get back to work."

Thomas extended his hand and Mr. Logan accepted it. They didn't shake, but instead held tight and nodded to each other.

Jebediah pushed on the bedroom door, and it bumped into something. He looked around to see what it hit. "Liz, what are you doing...listening through the door?"

The girl scowled at her father. "I wasn't listening,

Papa! I was looking for you and heard your voice."

"Git yourself in the other room!" The door slammed behind him.

Thomas couldn't imagine what the exchange between Elizabeth and her father was all about. He let his mind drift. His thoughts went straight away to Margaret. He now understood why the young woman hated him so. He represented everything bad in her life. "O Lord, I pray Ye'd take away the poor lass's pain. I beg Yer forgiveness for my presence causing hurt to her even more. Please heal her brokenness, Father. In Yer Son's name, I pray."

Thomas grieved for Margaret's pain, knowing all too well how it felt to lose someone close. He was alone and isolated from his family so very far away. Thoughts of his mother and sister caused a wave of sorrow to wash over him. *Was there nothing I could have done to save them, Lord? Oh, Father, I don't deserve the kindness I've been shown here. I couldn't save my mam and dear little Elizabeth…Lord, please show me what I can do to help heal Margaret's heart.*

7

The house shook and windows rattled.

Margaret flew through the kitchen door. "Mama, do you have any idea where Elizabeth is? Papa asked us to do some work in the garden, and I can't find her anywhere."

"I have no idea where she is, Margaret. Last I saw, she was in your bedroom at the writing desk, but that was hours ago." She raised the knife to continue peeling the potatoes.

June and Jeremiah ran through the door with outstretched arms and tearful faces.

Mama lifted the knife high in the air when the two youngest children grabbed her around the legs.

The cannons blasting away in the Gulf would give panic to the strongest of constitutions.

Mama dropped both the knife and potato into the dry sink and wrapped her arms around her two little ones. She inched toward the kitchen table and sat down to pull the children onto her lap. "All right now, don't fret. You're all in one piece, aren't you?" She playfully poked around on their sides. Laughter broke through their sobs. "You both feel fine to me."

June slid off Mama's lap. Indignant hands clamped onto tiny hips. "Don't tickle us, Mama. Me and Jer'miah is scared to death." June was probably ten percent serious and ninety percent playacting. It was most likely a ploy to shirk her assignment of watching baby Jeremiah while dinner was prepared.

Jeremiah continued to cry, and Margaret knew he wasn't pretending.

Mama pressed his head against her bosom and rocked back and forth, shushing him. "I understand you're scared, and I know it sounds frightening, but those old ships out there in the Gulf aren't firing at us. They're shooting at each other. Now tell me, has our house ever been hit by one of those cannon balls?"

"Don't tease me, Mama. You know Lizbeth found that big ol' cannon ball right in the middle of our cotton field. She said it coulda hit any one of us square in the head and knocked us plumb cuckoo."

*Of course she would remember that...*she remembered everything. Margaret wanted to laugh but stopped when Mama pointed her finger at June.

"You better watch that sassy mouth of yours, Miss Priss."

"Yes, ma'am." June hung her head.

Mama looked up at Margaret. "You know, if I had my way, I'd put both President Davis and President Lincoln in a room and deprive them of any and all modern conveniences until they settled their differences without one more drop of bloodshed." She hugged her baby tight. "But I suppose that won't happen any time soon." She covered Jeremiah's ear with her hand as she raised her voice. "Elizabeth! I need you in the kitchen. Where could that girl be?" Mama picked up a cup towel from the table and wiped her hands.

"You know good and well she's probably flittin' around somewhere...up to no good," June said.

Mama gave June a warning look.

You're one smart little girl, June Marie, probably right too. Margaret kept those thoughts to herself. "I told you, Mama. She's nowhere to be found."

Another blast of cannon fire tore through the air and this time, Jeremiah wailed.

Margaret felt terrible for Mama. The bowl of unpeeled potatoes and the ingredients for cornbread were forgotten. A labored sigh escaped her mama's lips, and she paused a moment before handing Margaret the baby boy. She put her hands on June's shoulders and turned her toward the kitchen door. "Margaret, I'm sorry, but I need you more than your papa does right now. Take these two young'uns to the front room and see if you can't distract them until I get dinner made or this war's over...whichever comes first."

"Mama, when is Elizabeth going to start doing her share of the work around here?"

Mama exhaled a long breath as she nudged the two girls toward the door. "Margaret, please, just do this for me, and I'll take care of your sister when and if she decides to show up for dinner."

Margaret pursed her lips as Mama returned to the sink. She wiped her brow and picked up another potato as Margaret ducked around the corner and into the front room.

The back screen door flew open and Papa made his presence known in the kitchen. "Where in the world are Margaret and Elizabeth? I gave them a job to do and they've up and disappeared. What in tarnation is going on around here? When I give an order, I expect it to be followed, Caroline."

Margaret leaned against the wall that ran between the front room and the kitchen. She lowered her baby brother to the floor and he toddled to June. The little actress was lying flat on her back on the big oval rug, pretending to be a forlorn princess banished to the Tower of London.

"Jebediah, don't go blaming Margaret." Mama's voice came slow and even. "She told me you had chores for them and she's been looking for Elizabeth too. We don't know where that girl is. And I'm the one who asked Margaret to help me so I can get dinner ready. Now come on in here and have a seat."

A kitchen chair scraped the floor. One of the cabinets creaked as it was opened. Water flowed and a low clank meant the coffee pot was being put on the stove.

A particularly loud cannon blast shook the house.

"Father, Your protection over this family." Mama called out for divine help.

Jeremiah screamed and raised his hands in the air before he toddled to Margaret.

She scooped him up and patted his back.

June raised her head from the rug.

Margaret put a finger to her lips, warning her sister to remain silent, while she soothed Jeremiah.

June's eyes rolled back and she sighed, letting her head fall to the rug with a thump.

Something that sounded like her father's fist hit the table with a loud bang. "That's it. I'm going to the coast to see what's happening down there." A chair slid back.

"There's nothing you can do over there but get yourself killed. Now sit down and have a cup of coffee."

"Caroline...what are we going to do about Elizabeth? She's getting more disobedient as each day passes."

The strong aroma of fresh coffee floated out of the kitchen.

"I don't know, Jeb." There was a long pause. "Here we are in the middle of a war and she's gone missing. I don't know if I should be worried sick or mad as a hornet!"

"I'm leaning toward the mad side myself," Papa said.

Mama gave a low laugh.

"The other day I caught her eavesdropping on my conversation with Thomas! I don't know what's got into that gal."

Margaret's eyebrows rose. If Papa caught her eavesdropping, he'd be upset. She had not done so intentionally; her parents were talking rather loudly and she couldn't help but hear. Still, she was in the wrong. *Please forgive me, Father.*

A cabinet door opened and something big clanked. More thumping was heard and then another chair was pulled out. Mama must have been moving her potato peeling to the table. "It seems like things have gone from bad to worse since we brought Thomas here."

"Aw, I don't know that he has anything to do with it. I hate to say it, but she's starting to act just like Emma used to."

"Don't talk like that," Mama snapped at Papa. "Elizabeth isn't in her condition."

Who were they talking about?

"I'm sorry, hon." Papa paused before changing his tune. "Well, maybe she's starting to...you know."

She heard Mama drop a potato into the bowl. "What, get her monthly?"

"Caroline, hold your tongue, there are three men

living in this house, for goodness sakes!"

Margaret clamped her hand over her mouth to hold in the laugh trying to escape.

"Jebediah Logan, for as long as you've been living in a house full of women, you should be used to our ways by now. Besides, you're the only *man* in this house right now. Jeremiah is just a baby, and Mr. Murphy is out piddling around in the garden."

"So what do you think about our Mr. Murphy?"

"And just what do you mean by that?"

"I was just wondering how you feel about him. You know he's had a hard life—even before he came to America."

"Oh, how's that?"

"Well, you cutting those potatoes made me think about him telling me how he lost some of his family in that horrible potato famine we read about."

"It's a cruel world we live in, Jeb. I only hope some good will come of this war—somehow." Another potato dropped into the bowl. "I don't know about you, but I've taken a liking to Thomas. I've even thought—"

Cannon fire exploded, drowning her parents' voices. Jeremiah wailed and Margaret hugged him to her.

"...our Margaret."

"I don't think that will be as hard as you think, darling." Papa chuckled.

Margaret wanted to run into the kitchen and demand to be told what had been said about her, but of course she didn't.

The front door opened.

"Elizabeth, where on earth have you been? Papa gave us a chore to do hours ago and you just up and disappeared." Cross with her sister, Margaret patted Jeremiah's back.

Mama and Papa came into the front room.

"Stop exaggerating, Margaret. It hasn't been hours." Elizabeth's words came back with fury. "Besides, it's none of your business where I've been."

"Well, it may not be Margaret's business, but it certainly is mine, young lady," Mama said.

Papa stood strong behind her.

"Yes, ma'am." Elizabeth shrank at Mama's stern words and her bottom lip quivered as tears rolled down her cheeks.

"Where have you been?"

"I went over to Mr. and Mrs. Milton's place to check if they had any eggs for sale. I was just trying to help out, Mama."

"How were you going to get eggs without any money?" Margaret asked.

"I thought I'd see if they had some before I asked you for money." Elizabeth glared at Margaret before turning back to Mama.

"Well, did they have any?" Mama asked.

"I...I...no! They didn't have any extras today." She wrung her hands.

"I think I know where you were, and it wasn't at the Miltons' getting eggs. Now..."

June appeared with Jeremiah in tow. She tugged on Mama's skirt. "See, Mama, I told you Lizbeth was up to no good, and I was right."

"Mama?" Elizabeth stood with her arms opened wide.

Margaret wanted to laugh at June's comment, but it wasn't the right time.

Papa intervened, taking June by the hand. "Come

on, girl. You're right in the line of fire." He picked Jeremiah up and then led June into the kitchen.

"Elizabeth, you've lied to me and your papa one too many times. I suggest you suck up those alligator tears, march yourself into your room, and do some serious business with the Lord. I'll be in later to issue your punishment."

"But, Mama—"

"Not another word."

Elizabeth clenched her fists and stomped off.

"What has gotten into her?" Margaret asked.

Mama didn't answer. She smoothed her hair back and released another long breath of air before heading to the kitchen.

Papa sat at the table with both of the little ones perched on his knees.

"Mama, I'm hungry." June fiddled with one of the potatoes still waiting to be peeled.

Mama looked heavenward. She slid the paring knife out of the little girl's reach. "June, it's been a while since I've heard any cannon fire. Can you take Jeremiah out on the front porch to play?"

The little girl slid off Papa's knee. "I guess so." She helped the baby down and led him toward the door. "Come on, Jer'miah. Mama wants us out of here so she can talk to Papa about what Lizbeth did."

Margaret met Papa's gaze. He burst into laughter, causing her to giggle.

"All right, you two. The last thing she needs is you encouraging her." Mama sat down to finish peeling the potatoes.

Margaret put her hand over her mouth, not wanting to anger Mama any further. Papa picked up his coffee mug. He placed it in the sink and moved behind Mama. He bent over and put his arms around her. He whispered something in her ear.

Mama laid her head over on his arm. "I love you too. I just don't understand why things have to be so hard. Can't there be one good thing come out of this old war? I don't know how to deal with Elizabeth. Why is she acting this way?"

"I don't know, honey, but I think we ought to pray about it before we talk to her."

"I agree." She resumed peeling when Papa released her.

"Margaret, you can start the work Papa gave you."

"Yes, Mama." Margaret was deep in thought as she walked outside. *What did Papa mean? "She's acting just like Emma." Who on earth was Emma? And what was her condition they spoke of?* She knew it hadn't been right to listen to what Mama and Papa were saying, especially after Papa's remark about Elizabeth's eavesdropping, but now that she had, she had plenty to ponder. She reached the small garden plot and what she saw made fiery anger well up inside her.

8

"What do you think you're doing in our garden?" Margaret hiked up her skirt and climbed over the short chicken-wire fence, placed there to protect the garden from small pests, including a few displaced sand crabs. Her leg brushed against a sharp edge, cutting into her knee. She winced in pain and grabbed the wound, spilling her apronful of seeds in the process. She gritted her teeth, unable to determine if she was angrier at the seeds falling or at Thomas Murphy standing in their garden.

Thomas leaned against the hoe.

"You should not be here, Mr. Murphy. You need to return to your bedroom before someone sees you."

"It looks like ye might have hurt your leg, lass. Would ye like for me to take a look at it?" Thomas ignored her angry tone.

Margaret gasped and clapped her hands down onto her skirt. "You'll do no such thing."

"Yer papa gave me permission to work in the garden...said it would be a great help to him."

Margaret turned, irritated at how calm he appeared when she was madder than a wet hen. She dropped to the ground where the seeds had fallen.

Thomas knelt down beside her and helped gather them.

Margaret arose from the ground and dumped the

seeds out onto Papa's makeshift wooden table and began sorting, grudgingly acknowledging in her mind that he'd been most helpful, even though she still didn't like him and had made that plain to him. She paused for a moment and glanced up.

Thomas had worked the soil, his hoed rows perfectly even. His tall, broad shoulders barely fit in one of Papa's shirts. His dark hair was tied back with a string, accentuating his jawline. He was the epitome of manliness, not embarrassed to work the soil, as if firm in the conviction of where God placed him on this earth. He looked confident...the way a good husband should.

She turned back to the seed table, ashamed of gawking with the brazen desire of still wanting a husband, despite her Jeffrey now lying in the cold ground. Anger welled up against the object of her yearning. "Mr. Murphy...I rue the day I ever set eyes on you." She didn't raise her head from the pile of seeds.

Thomas stopped working the ground to rub his injured shoulder. The action of hoeing must be causing a great amount of pain.

"Does your shoulder hurt?" She looked at him. "I hope those soldiers' bullets hurt you like your people have hurt our southern way of life." She huffed out a breath. "You're probably one of those fool Yankees who think the war is about freeing the slaves. For heaven's sake, what's it to you if a few southerners own slaves to help out with their farms?" Margaret completely abandoned the seeds and turned to face the man.

"Miss Margaret, I've felt my fair share of pain because of this war, but you know what, I'd do it all over again if it would help to free the slaves. Now there's a people who have suffered a great deal more than you and I will ever know. Ye might know that if ye'd ever taken the chance to talk to one of them."

Margaret felt her cheeks warm. "Do you really think those Negroes care one way or another? Besides, if they *were* given their freedom, they would probably run back to their masters lickety-split because they wouldn't even know how to survive on their own."

Thomas gave her a look of disdain and shook his head. "I know you only speak from ignorance, but if ye knew the truth about the Negro people, you would be telling a far different story, to be sure, lass."

"If anyone around here is ignorant, it would be you, Mr. Murphy! If you had any sense at all, you would know that the North doesn't care one bit about the Negroes. All they want is to lord their power over the South!" She clenched her fists on the seed table. "If anything, the North is using the slaves as an excuse to cover up their real agenda...tyranny."

"Aye, yer Papa had much of the same opinions about the war. But no matter what ye think is the cause behind it, you've got to admit that owning another human being is not the Christian thing to do, lass." Thomas's eyes softened.

Margaret whipped her head back in astonishment that this man, a stranger, a foreigner...a Yankee, would dare question her Christian values. "Well. Why don't you tell me, Mr. Murphy, if slavery is so bad, then why is it talked about between the pages of the Bible?"

Thomas paused. "Have ye ever sang the song 'Amazing Grace'?"

"Of course I have! Before we moved to this godforsaken peninsula, my family belonged to one of the most respected Christian churches in New Orleans."

"Did ye know the song was written by the captain of a slave ship?"

"No, I did not. But that just proves my point. Anyone who could write a song like 'Amazing Grace' had to be an upstanding Christian man."

"Aye, he was, but not at the beginning. He was once a cruel, vile man who treated no one with respect, especially not the slaves in his care. The song tells a bit about his harrowing experience in a fierce storm and how God saw fit to deliver him through it. The verse says, 'Through many dangers, toils, and snares I have already come; 'tis grace that brought me safe thus far and grace will lead me home.'"

"I don't understand what you're trying to say. It sounds to me as if this great man of faith had no problem with the slave trade."

"Well, lass, I don't know why he didn't immediately quit what he was doing, but I do know that many years after his conversion, he admitted to how sorry he was, and he supported the abolition of slavery in Great Britain."

"That's all well and good, but you still haven't answered my question. If it was OK for the people in the Bible to own slaves, why is it wrong for the South to own them today?"

"Miss Margaret, surely ye remember the story of Moses delivering the children of Israel from the hands of the Egyptian pharaoh. God commanded him to do it because He'd heard the anguished cries of His people. They were sorely oppressed slaves under their masters and begged for deliverance. Don't ye think the Negroes feel the same way?" Thomas's words were spoken with peace.

Margaret was drawn into his way of thinking, to what he said. But she couldn't give in quite yet. "But, that's different! Those were God's chosen people, and they didn't deserve to be slaves to the pharaoh."

"So yer saying the African people deserve to be slaves?"

"Why don't you just mind your own business and go back inside the house before some foot soldier sees you and drags your Yankee tail end to the fort!"

Thomas put his hand over hers.

Margaret wanted to yank it away, but his touch was much too wonderful to resist.

"Miss Margaret, yer papa told me all the horrible things you've been through. I know all about how ye had to up and leave yer home in New Orleans. And I know about ye losing yer fiancé. I...I just want to tell you how very sorry I am for the pain my presence must be causin' ye. I would do anything to ease yer burden."

His lovely, lyrical voice, the way he spoke those words, was like a soothing balm to her heart and yet they also burned like salt in a fresh wound. Part of her wanted to fall into his warm embrace and sob for all she'd lost. But he was a Yankee, the cause of her loss. She jerked her hand away. "Mr. Murphy, you've never felt pain like I have." Her voice sounded bitter, even to her.

"Aye, but I've felt plenty of pain in my life and..."

Tears welled up. Giving him the pleasure of seeing her cry wasn't something she would allow. "I don't want to hear anything more you have to say!" She hiked up her skirt and leapt over the fence, running down the long trail toward the bay.

"Miss Margaret, wait. I'm sorry. Please don't run away!"

The sounds of the bay and a long walk would help soothe her bitter soul. She only hoped there weren't any more injured Union soldiers to run into on her way. And he wouldn't dare take the chance of following after her.

9

Margaret's heart pounded. The farther she ran from Thomas Murphy, the better she felt. The wind stung her cheeks, which already burned with the anger inside her.

Whitecaps bounced on the bay in tune with the swaying breeze, unaware of her bruised ego. Her bare feet sank into soft sand at the edge of the dunes. The roof of the Stoltze place came into view. She slowed her pace. Her cheeks were wet from the tears she'd shed. Pulling the apron to her face, she wiped them away. *Stupid Yankee! What could he possibly know about my pain...or about the slaves...or why the South went to war in the first place? He doesn't know anything.* "O Lord, how can I hate someone so much and at the same time want him to hold me in his arms and protect me? Father God, why have You done this to me? Haven't I been through enough?"

She covered her face with her betraying hands that had loved his touch. Her embittered weeping was interrupted by a sweet sound floating over the dunes. She got back on her feet and wiped away the tears. Someone was singing.

"Roll, Jerdan, roll. Roll, Jerdan, roll.
I want'ta go to heav'n when I die, to hear ol' Jerdan roll!
O brethren,
Roll, Jerdan, roll. Roll, Jerdan, roll.

I want'ta go to heav'n when I die, to hear ol' Jerdan roll! Sing it ova now…!"

Beautiful, dark-skinned Necie, the Stoltzes' slave girl, sat on a short wooden stool, hunched over a washtub. She scrubbed her master's clothes with the smooth side of a seashell.

Thomas had said she'd never taken the time to talk to a Negro.

Rubbish! I've waved and said hello to Necie at least a dozen times. Margaret smoothed down her skirt and apron and walked toward the young woman. Unlike the other times she'd seen Necie, she decided not to just wave hello and go on. This time, she'd take notice.

The girl was around her own age. The cotton blouse and skirt Necie wore hadn't known their original color for some time.

Margaret stepped on a stick and broke it underfoot, making her presence known.

Necie's song came to a halt. Her gaze darted around before landing on Margaret. "Miss Margaret? What you doin' wanderin' round out here on the beach? You done scared me half to death! You know it ain't safe for a purdy girl like you to be out here alone."

Margaret's cheeks warmed. "Hello, Necie."

"You all right, Miss Margaret? Looks like you been crying."

"Oh, it's nothing. Tell me, how's Mrs. Stoltze doing these days?" Margaret covered her embarrassment with questions.

Necie shook her head. "Oh, Miss Margaret, she ain't doin' so good. She got the rheumatism in her hands so bad they's no more than crab claws anymore." Necie mimicked how the elderly woman's hands moved. "She don't walk too good neither. Her backbone so twisted up…" She shook her head again and dragged the seashell over the shirt she was washing. "Come winter time, she probably ain't goin' to be able to get outta bed at all."

Margaret thought to tell Mama to check on the elderly couple soon. She sat on the sturdy driftwood log next to the girl. "Necie…Mr. and Mrs. Stoltze bought you from the slave trader after Mrs. Stoltze's sickness made her unable to keep up with her chores, isn't that right?"

"Yes'm, that's right. She's a mighty sick woman and Massa Stoltze ain't much better off than her. They so old." Necie laughed. "Sometime Massa Stoltze can't even remember where he's at."

Oh dear, that doesn't sound good at all. "Tell me, Necie, how do Mr. and Mrs. Stoltze treat you?"

"Now what make you want to ask a question like that for, Miss Margaret?"

"I was just wondering if they…well, you know…have they ever beat you?" Margaret fiddled with the hem of her apron.

Necie flung her head back and laughed. "Oh, no! They treats me real good, Miss Margaret. Besides, they so old they can't even beat eggs, much less me!"

"Well, tell me then, what is it that's so bad about being a slave?"

The young girl moistened her lips and her cheerful laughter faded. "Well, I s'pose the worst thing I can ever remember is when I was sold away from my family back in Louisiana." Necie rubbed the seashell back and forth over the shirt in her washtub. Her mind appeared to have gone far away.

"I'm sorry to hear that." Margaret too had been

made to leave her home. She at least had her family to comfort her though.

Necie had no one. But if that was normal for a slave, then that was the way it had to be.

"My Moses and me was plannin' to jump the broomstick fo I got drug off."

"Jump the broomstick? What do you mean?"

"Miss Margaret, you know slaves can't get married like white folk can. It ain't legal. So when slaves fall in love and wanna get hitched, we just jump over the broomstick together to show everybody we's married."

This young woman had lived in Louisiana...just as Margaret had. And she was to be married...just as Margaret had planned. Her dreams had been dashed on the rocks of life as surely as Margaret's own.

"Ye might know that if ye'd ever taken the chance to talk to one of them."

Thomas's words stung deep in her heart. What he said about the slaves was true. It hurt all the more to admit that she knew very little about slavery. There was a more important reason than just states' rights that the war was being fought. And even with all the modern resources available for a person to learn, she'd never taken the initiative to find out. She crossed her arms over her churning stomach as the young woman continued.

"We wanted to get married cause I's gonna have Moses's baby."

Shocked, Margaret's instinct was to gasp and slap her hand over her mouth, but she made a concerted effort to control her actions.

"Life was hard for the menfolk working at the sugarcane plantation. I's thankful I don't have to work in that boilin' house where they melt down the sugar. My Moses work in there keepin' the fires going all day, every day. It so hot your skin feel like it gonna drop off your bones. But I got to work in the big house taking care of the missy's little ones." A smile crept across her face. "They little, white-haired babies be so sweet…not like the massa." The edges of Necie's mouth turned down. Her brown eyes closed to slits.

"What happened? Did the master beat you?" Margaret watched as tears began to roll down Necie's face. She shouldn't have made her dredge up such painful memories.

"No! He sold me away so I can't be with my Moses. I fight hard so I don't has to leave my mammy and my Moses. I kick and I scratch that man so he thinks I's so bad he don't want to take me with him." Her bottom lip trembled and her voice squeaked. "But then he kicked me so hard and I fell down and can't get back up. He just scoop me up and throwed me into the wagon and drive away with my mammy layin' with her face on the ground bawlin' and squallin'. Down the road a ways, I started to hurt so bad in my belly. I look down and sees blood all over my skirt and all over the floor of that wagon. My baby died and I passed him right there in the back of that wagon on my way to Texas."

Margaret couldn't hold back her tears. She'd held her dead baby brother, Jeremiah's twin, when Mama wasn't able to. And, oh, how hard it had been when it came time to give him back to the Lord. The memory was painful and it wasn't even her child. She couldn't imagine the pain and loneliness Necie must have felt. "Oh, Necie, how can you stand it? My fiancé is dead, but the man you love is still alive and you're not allowed to be with him."

Necie wiped her tears on the towel she had draped over her shoulder. "My heart hurt for a long, long time. But I can't stay sad about it. Mrs. Stoltze told me about Jesus and how when I get to heaven, my baby boy's gonna be there waiting for me. She say Jesus was God's little boy, and He love me so much He gave His Son to die for me, and if I believe in Him, I's gonna go to heaven when I die. I got faith He gonna do what He say He gonna do." Necie's words of God's grace seemed to soothe her and give her back her smile.

It was incomprehensible to Margaret how this young woman managed to go on living after what she'd been through. Guilt and shame washed over her and made her feel sick. What kind of Christian was she that a slave had more faith in God than she did?

Necie wrung water from the shirt she'd so thoroughly scrubbed and placed it on a rock beside the washtub. As she fished for another piece of clothing, she began humming the tune of the song she'd been singing earlier.

"Necie, what is that song you were singing? I've never heard it before." Margaret wiped the tears from her face.

"Oh, it's a slave song they sings back on the plantation. My mammy sing it all the time. Mrs. Stoltze say it talk about the River Jordan in her Bible where them Israelites crossed over to get to the Promised Land. She say it also the river where Jesus got baptized. I know she right, 'cause Mrs. Stoltze sure know her Bible." She didn't look at Margaret as she shook her head. "But back on the plantation they say it a song about a river up north where a slave can cross over and be free."

"Why would they sing a song about the Jordan River if it was really about escaping their masters?"

"Now, Miss Margaret, if they sing about running away where the massa can hear, they all gonna get a whoopin'."

Margaret gasped. "Oh, I suppose you're right about that."

"But for me, I wanna believe that song is really about that Jordan River they talk about in the Bible. I know I never gonna run away. There nowhere to run to on this ol' peninsula. What's I gonna do, swim away?" She gave a contagious smile. "I just stay with Massa and Miss Stoltze and pray someday my Jesus gonna deliver me to the Promised Land."

Margaret was amazed at how Necie could have any faith at all in the midst of such a hopeless situation, but somehow...with Jesus Christ as her Lord and Savior...she was able to overcome.

How had she not understood before? The Bible said God had made man in His own image. Not just the white men—all men. Slowly, the idea sank in. A Negro was capable of having feelings like anyone else. To think she'd believed what a few people had said...that Negroes were soulless like the animals.

Oh, Lord, how could I have been so ignorant? Of course Necie has a soul...a loving and caring soul. And a good heart that loves unconditionally...not like me, putting provisions on everyone. Oh, Father, please, please forgive me! The Lord's cleansing forgiveness came as suddenly as the words had poured from her heart. She rose from the driftwood log and put her arms around Necie in a long embrace. She didn't deserve the soft patting she felt on her back, but it comforted her to know she'd made a new friend.

"Goodbye, Miss Margaret. Tell yo sista, Miss Elizabeth, I says hello."

Margaret was taken by surprise. "Elizabeth has been here?"

"She come by here earlier today. She come by all the time when she goin' up to the Langley place. Sometime I be outside tending to our vegetables and she come by and say hello."

So that's where she's been going. "Goodbye, Necie. I'll have Mama come by and check on Mr. and Mrs. Stoltze soon." Margaret waved as she walked away from Necie's washing place. She wanted to feel the cool water around her feet and the soft, squishy sand beneath them. There was much she needed to think about on her way back home.

So many things had happened in such a short span of time. Everything she'd known as truth about the slaves and the reasons for the war had changed. Thomas had been right. He understood so much more than she. *Maybe the Yankees aren't such horrible people after all. Maybe Thomas isn't the monster I've made him out to be. Maybe it's OK that I have...feelings for him.*

Her mind drifted to what Necie had said about Elizabeth. *How long has she been going up to the Langley place? There is no reason for her to be there.* Both of Widower Langley's sons went off to fight in the war. Only one came back, and he was one of the hard cases. The war left him limbless, save for one arm, and that wasn't the worst of it. *What kind of business would Elizabeth have with an old man who hates everyone on earth and his son, who doesn't even know he lives on earth? Dear Lord, help us all.*

10

Thomas told Mr. Logan what happened between him and Margaret, but the man already knew, admitting he and Mrs. Logan had seen the whole exchange from the kitchen window. Thomas searched through the shed for the tool he needed, deciding the work would keep his mind off Margaret. *Forgive me, Lord, and protect her, please...*

He checked the old saw's sharpness and returned to the work at hand. The piece of wood had been used many times before, judging by the nail holes scarring its rough grain. But even scraps of wood had to be reused. Supplies were a scarce commodity, especially wood. He searched for the right-sized piece of driftwood to use, but the hunt was fruitless.

"Beeehhhh-eh-eh-eh-eh-eh!"

"Hush now, Nanny Sue. I'll have yer pen fixed up nice and new before ye know it and then ye won't have to be tied up anymore."

Thomas talked to the goat as if she understood what he said. He'd done the daily milking since regaining his strength. But Nanny Sue's milk was beginning to dry up. They'd need to breed her soon if they were to have milk in the coming year. He would have to discuss their options with Mr. Logan.

Thomas overheard Mrs. Logan talk about trading some of the fall vegetables to Mr. Milton in exchange for a pair of chickens so they would have their own source of eggs and eventually a nice chicken dinner. Images of baked poultry floated through Thomas's head.

He knelt and rested the plank across his knee to saw it. That was another chore. He would make some hay bales directly after finishing the goat pen.

It eased Thomas's mind that he could repay their kindness in giving him lodging and caring for him during his recovery. He couldn't understand the abundant generosity of the Logan family. Surely God had brought him to this place for a reason.

The grass rustled behind him. Someone was coming.

He instinctively picked up the saw for protection. A glimpse of raven hair came into view. Thomas dipped his head in acknowledgement of her presence and carried on with his work.

She leaned against the shed, watching him.

Thomas retrieved a hammer. He returned to the goat pen, picked up the broken piece of wood, and pulled the nails holding the chicken wire in place. *Oh, Lord, did Ye hear my prayer? Did Ye work on her heart?*

"Good afternoon, Mr. Murphy."

"Good afternoon, Miss Margaret. Ye know, lass, I'm fine with ye calling me Thomas, if you'd like."

"All right then…Thomas, I was wondering if you might have time to talk."

The sound of his name on her lips was indeed a pleasure. He put down the hammer and rose, trying his best not to show the pain from his still healing body. "Of course. I'd be happy to talk to ye."

"Can you come out back? I don't want little ears listening in."

He couldn't be sure, but Thomas sensed a break in the ice. He followed her as quickly as the rainbow follows the rain.

Margaret made her way to the back of the property. When she came upon a felled log, she sat on it, facing the saltwater slough at the back of the Logan land.

Thomas joined her, careful to keep his distance. He surveyed the property. No one was within earshot.

"Thomas…" A long pause followed as she plucked a lone sea-oat stem and twirled it between her fingers. "I…I'd like to apologize to you."

Oh, forgive me, Father. Why do I never seem to expect an answer when I pray? Thomas touched her hand. "What on earth for, lass?"

Margaret didn't look at him. "You were right, and I was wrong."

"About what, Miss Margaret?"

"I took your advice and talked to a slave. A slave I've always known, but never took the time to talk to." Her body began to shake. She lowered her face into her hands. "And you were so right—slavery is awful!"

Thomas inched closer and put his arm around her. "There, there now, lass." To his surprise, she didn't withdraw. Even more unexpected, she turned toward him and continued her cry on his shoulder. He never wanted to let go of her.

"It's OK, Miss Margaret. How could ye know how bad slavery is when ye have never seen it first-hand?"

Margaret wiped her tears with her apron. "But now I know how horrible it is. And to think, I've hated the Union all these years for no good reason. If they actually are fighting against slavery, then they fight for a noble cause."

"Aye now, but ye did have a good reason for your feelings. After all, yer fiancé died at the hands of the Union army. That would cause anyone to have hatred in their heart."

"I don't know what to feel anymore. I'm so confused. Everything I've always believed as truth doesn't seem to make sense anymore. Why does God let these things happen, Thomas?"

He folded his arms and watched a seagull take wing and fly across the slough. "I've asked myself that many a time after what happened to my family and my homeland. There was so much death and betrayal and people unwilling to help their fellow man. It's enough to make anyone question God."

"Oh, my heavens, you know so much about me and I hardly know a thing about you. Please tell me about your family…about Ireland."

This sudden interest in him thrilled Thomas, and excitement filled his heart as he turned and straddled the log so he could face her. "Goodness, where do I start? I suppose you know about the great hunger in Ireland."

"Oh yes, Papa read the story in the paper to Mama and me. Such a horrible thing."

"After my baby sister, Elizabeth, died from the fever, Mam didn't last very long after that. I've a feeling she starved herself to death so we could eat."

Margaret clasped her hands over her mouth. She was going to cry again. "You lost your mama and your sister? That's so sad, Thomas. Were they all you had?" Tears streamed down her face.

"No, I still had my pap and two brothers. We were just boys then. Not as feisty as we once were due to the famine. But nevertheless, we had to bury our dead.

And since we had no money, we were evicted from our cottage and had nowhere to go."

Margaret wiped her cheek with the back of her hand. "What did you do?"

"Like so many other homeless families, we were put on boats and promised five pounds from an agent when we arrived at our destination. Fifty-three days later, we found ourselves in Montreal, Canada.

"Oh, lass, it was a horrible trip indeed with all the fever, retching, and dysentery. I had no idea how bad things really were until we got off the boat and saw my dead countrymen stacked like cordwood on the banks of the St. Lawrence. And, of course, there was no agent to be found. It was just a story we were told. So we were put into temporary shacks with loads of other families, or what was left of them."

Margaret wiped her cheeks and put her hand over his. "It must have been awful for you. How could you possibly bear it?"

Thomas slid his other hand on top of hers. "I don't think I would be here today, had it not been for a missionary by the name of Leeland Montgomery. He said he heard about what the Irish had been through and came from New York City to help. Bless him, he brought hearty soup and bread and nursed as many of us as he could back to health. Then he shared the gospel with us and I learned the true love of God. That night, our bellies were filled with the milk of human kindness and our souls were filled with the Spirit."

"You mean you didn't know Jesus before then...what about your mama and baby sister?"

"After the famine and their deaths, I decided I didn't want anything to do with religion. So yes, my mam and sister are safe in Jesus's arms, but in my pain and anger I refused to believe. Praise God, Mr. Montgomery found me when he did. I've been serving the Lord ever since."

She rubbed his hand. "Thank you for sharing your story with me, Thomas. It's amazing how you can be so cheerful of heart after having been through so much in your life."

"Aye, it's the grace of God, lass."

"So how did you end up in America?"

"After we regained our strength, Pap refused to live under British rule another day, so the four of us walked all the way from Canada to New York." Thomas enjoyed the dimples that graced her cheeks when she smiled.

"And now you're an Irish Yankee living in the Deep South."

"I can't imagine a nicer place to live, lass. If it weren't for you and yer folks, I'd probably be dead on that beach." He gestured toward the bay. "Thankfully, yer mama and papa are good, God-fearing people with love for their fellow man. They seem to do everything right."

"What do you mean?"

Thomas looked longingly into her violet eyes. "Well, they certainly have raised a mighty wonderful and beautiful daughter."

Color rose in Margaret's cheeks. Her hand went to her throat.

He'd embarrassed her, and for that, he was sorry.

She rose from the log. "I really must get in the house. I'm sure Mama will be needing my help soon."

"Wait, I'm sorry. I didn't mean to cause ye any pain."

"No, no, it's all right. I just need to go inside for

now."

"Please forgive me, lass."

"There's nothing to forgive, Thomas…really. And thank you for sharing with me about your family. I just need time to think through some things." Margaret walked toward the house.

There were chores he needed to tend to, but there was something far more important that needed done first. He sat back down on the log and bowed his head. *Father God, I know everything Ye do is for a purpose, and I know Yer the one who brought me here. I'm so thankful You've given me yet another chance at life and the opportunity to help these fine people with their land. Now, I don't claim to know everything You'd have me do, Lord, but I do know I'm falling hard for Miss Margaret Logan. I've never felt this way about a woman before, and I need Ye to lead me in how I am to proceed with her. Father, if it'd be Yer will, would Ye show me the right way to court this lovely lass? And bless my father and brothers too. In Yer Son's name…amen.*

Nanny Sue was bleating loud enough to wake the dead.

"I'm a comin', girl. I'm a comin'." Thomas pushed off the log to finish his work.

11

"OK, it's time to go now, June."

The little girl dramatically let her head flop back, rolled her eyes, and huffed out a long sigh. "Oh, Mama, I just sat down here to play with Jer'miah." She gestured toward her baby brother.

He cooed at his sister as he chewed on a wooden block.

"You're always wantin' me to play with Jer'miah so you can get the housework done, and now that I'm finally doing it, you want me to go chasing…"

"Shhhhhh!" Mama cut off June's complaint. "Miss Priss, I don't need any of your backtalk."

"Yes, ma'am." The little girl headed toward the door. "Well, here I go." She gave Mama an irritated look.

Margaret couldn't help but smile at her melodramatic little sister.

"Thank you, June. Now…off you go." Mama waved her out the door.

The screen slammed shut.

Margaret joined Jeremiah on the floor.

Mama went to her rocking chair and picked up the mending basket.

Margaret handed Jeremiah a block he tossed at her. "So…what was that all about?"

Mama picked a dark blue cotton pinafore from the

basket. She held it up. "This fabric is still in good shape. I think with a few alterations I can make it into a nice pair of overalls for Jeremiah."

"You didn't answer my question, Mama." Margaret held Jeremiah's little hands and helped him stand.

Mama rummaged through her box of sewing supplies and removed a pair of scissors. "I don't think your papa would want his little boy having a layer of lace covering his shoulders. And, Margaret...every single thing that goes on around this house isn't your business. Understand me?"

Margaret felt her face grow warm. "Yes, ma'am."

After a moment of uncomfortable silence, Jeremiah tottered over to Mama's chair and laid his head down. "I guess it's that time, isn't it, son." She pulled the little one onto her lap and began rocking him. Within moments, Jeremiah was asleep. Mama held him out to Margaret.

Margaret took him to Mama and Papa's bed.

"I won't be able to finish the mending." Mama sighed. "I need to get supper ready."

The screen door banged against the frame.

"Mama," June called as she walked into the kitchen. "I stood at the edge of the property and watched Lizbeth till I couldn't see her no more."

"June, you need to talk much quieter. Margaret just put Jeremiah down for a nap."

"Oh, sorry, Mama."

Mama asked June a question, but Margaret couldn't hear what she said.

"No, Mama, she didn't go to the fort. She kept right on walking all the way down the road."

"I'm very proud of the good job you did," Mama

told June.

"Thank you. Can I have that biscuit and honey you promised me now?"

"You sure can. Let's go fetch you one."

Margaret came to the kitchen. "Mama...June...did I hear you two talking about spying on Elizabeth?"

"Be quiet, Margaret. It's a secret, and you don't know nothin' about it. Mama's giving me my biscuit!"

Mama took the biggest biscuit on the tray, sliced it open, and slathered the insides with honey. She then handed it to June.

"Mama, can I go outside and play in the garden?"

"Sure you can." Mama smiled at her.

"Mr. Murphy is working out there, so don't be a pest," Margaret called to her.

"I won't," June said with a mouth full of biscuit, skipping out the back door.

"Mama, if you wanted to know where Elizabeth has been running off to, you should have just asked me."

"Well, I guess I've been dealing with the wrong little spy."

~*~

"Mama, I'm worried about Elizabeth. I suppose I should have told you sooner."

"What is it, Margaret?"

"It all happened a few weeks ago when I stumbled across Thomas in the garden. I was still mad that you and Papa let him come here. We had a huge argument and I stormed off to the bay. Do you remember that happening?"

"I remember. You didn't see another soldier, did

you?" Mama picked up two eggs, a bowl, and a whisk and sat down at the kitchen table.

"No, I just needed to collect my thoughts...and cool my temper." Margaret scooped up the right amount of cornmeal for the cornbread she knew Mama would prepare for their meal. "Anyway, I came up on the Stoltze place and noticed Necie doing the wash."

"Oh, how are the Stoltzes doing?"

"It doesn't sound as if they're doing very well, Mama. I'm sorry I forgot to tell you sooner, but I told Necie you would come and check in on them."

"That's all right. I'll pay them a visit later this week." Mama tapped the egg on the edge of the bowl, splitting the shell.

"I talked to Necie about some things, and she told me that Elizabeth had come by earlier that day. She said Elizabeth comes by quite often...on her way to...the Widower Langley's place."

"What on earth is she doing going there?" Mama stared at Margaret, her expression startled.

"I don't know, Mama." Margaret shrugged. "Maybe she's helping Mr. Langley take care of his son."

"I suppose that could be the case, but why wouldn't she tell me about it?" Mama stirred the mixture. "It's not right, her sneaking off. She's keeping secrets...but why?"

They were silent for a bit.

"Mama, why does Mr. Langley's son act the way he does? He scares me half to death with the way he screams all the time. I don't even walk past that house anymore because he shouts those horrible words out the window every time anyone goes by. Is it because he's upset about losing his arm and legs?"

Mama shook her head. "No, honey, it's not that."

"Then what would make him act like that?"

"When they brought Johnny home, everything was fine. He'd lost his limbs, but at least he still had his life. Most of the boys fighting weren't so blessed." She ran the back of her hand across her forehead and sighed. "But then an infection set in and he took a high fever. Mrs. Wallace told me women came from all over the peninsula to try and help bring the fever down. And they finally did manage to cool him off, but it was already too late."

"What do you mean it was too late? He's still alive."

"Yes, but the brain can't handle being that hot, and now he's touched in the head."

"So he doesn't know what he's doing when he says that stuff?"

"No, I'm afraid not."

Sadness draped over Margaret like a heavy blanket. "Poor Mr. Langley, he's lost everything—his wife died, his other son died…"

"And now he's left to take care of Johnny on his own. Maybe we should take a lesson from Elizabeth and see what we can do to help."

"I know, Mama. I feel bad for thinking Elizabeth was up to no good." Margaret cringed inwardly from her silent accusations of Elizabeth shirking chores.

"I do too, baby. I do too."

Mama finished preparing the cornbread batter.

Margaret coated the cast-iron skillet with lard. She lit the stove to melt the fat before lighting the oven. "I need to talk to you about something, Mama."

"What is it, dear?" Mama poured the contents of the bowl into the warm skillet.

"Well, that day in the garden when Thomas and I had, um, words, he told me that I might understand how bad slavery was if I actually talked to a slave."

"Yes…and?"

"I told you I talked to Necie."

"Uh-huh, and what did she say?"

"She told me the Stoltzes treat her real nice."

"Mr. and Mrs. Stoltze are good people. I wouldn't expect they'd be mean to anyone."

"Yes, but then she told me how she ended up with Mr. and Mrs. Stoltze." Margaret sat down. "She had horrible things done to her before she came here. Did you know she was sold here from Louisiana just before she was going to jump the broom with a slave named Moses? Do you even know what that means, Mama?"

"Yes, I do know what jumping the broom means." Mama grabbed a chair and looked up at the ceiling before turning her attention back to Margaret. "Honey, slavery can be horrible. I saw firsthand how awful it was when you were just little bitty. Papa and I traveled into New Orleans to pick up supplies for the lighthouse at the French Quarter.

"He parked the buggy right next to the place on the river where they held the slave auctions. I stayed with you while he went in to pick up the packages. I'll never forget the pitiful wailing and weeping coming from the cages where they'd locked up the Negroes. They were told to line up so buyers could inspect them like cattle." Mama sat down in the chair. "There were three young girls up on the auction block. I was sure they were sisters by the way they clung to one another. One seemed to be your age and the two others, about Elizabeth's age, I would guess. They were pretty little things all dressed up in gingham dresses and bonnets.

I found out later the owners cleaned up the slaves and gave them nice clothes so they would bring more money at auction.

"Well, anyway, the oldest girl was sold to a local family as a nanny to their children. Then the two youngest girls were sold as a pair. The bidding went on for some time and ended with the girls being sold to a man from a sugar plantation way out in the country."

"So then what happened?"

"The whole time I sat there and watched those three young sisters being split up and sold, I heard a woman who was still in the cage hollering and crying as if someone was tearing her heart out.

"For the life of me I couldn't figure out what was wrong with her until the girls were called off the auction block." Mama released a labored breath. "They ran over to the woman and hugged her through that awful cage. Then I realized she was their mother and it probably did feel like her heart was being ripped out.

"After that I held you so tight to my bosom because I knew how I would feel if someone had tried to take you away from me. Suppose that was the last time she would ever see her children? When Papa returned to the buggy, I told him what I'd seen and we vowed right then to never have anything to do with slavery. I know we're taught here in the South that the Negroes aren't good for anything but hard labor, but I don't believe it." Mama sniffed and wiped her eye with the edge of her apron.

Margaret couldn't stop the flood of tears. "Why haven't you ever told me this before, Mama? Why didn't you or Papa tell us kids how bad slavery is? You just let us believe what anyone has ever said about the Negroes."

"Margaret! I assumed you would realize we don't condone the use of slaves. Papa refused to purchase any slaves to help with running the lighthouse. Your papa and I have always worked hard for what we have, without anyone's help. So I ask you...what would make you think we would support such a horrible institution?"

"Because, Mama, if we don't condone slavery then—then my Jeffrey died in vain."

Mama rushed to Margaret's side. She fell to her knees, swallowing her in a tight embrace. "Oh, Margaret, that's just not true. Jeffrey died fighting for the South's rights. You've got to believe *that*, honey." Mama wept now too.

"I don't know what to believe anymore. Everything I've ever believed in seems to have changed since Thomas came here." Margaret sobbed. "I'm so confused."

Mama softly patted her back. "All right now, we'll talk this whole thing out." She rose from her kneeling position and straightened her skirt. "But first we need a fresh pot of coffee."

"Mama...I need to tell you something and it can't wait for the pot to boil."

A look of deep concern washed over Mama's face. "What is it?"

"I think I'm falling in love with Thomas."

A smile crept across Mama's face. "Why don't you tell me something I don't already know?"

Margaret looked at her mama in complete disbelief.

"Close your mouth, dear. You'll catch flies."

"How could you possibly know my feelings about Thomas?"

"Because, dear..." Mama turned to her. "I believe in the power of prayer."

"You know...you can be a very confusing mama at times."

"Dear daughter, when Jeffrey died, it broke my heart too. I hurt so bad for you, and then when we moved away from New Orleans, you were torn up all the more. I've prayed every night since Jeffrey died that God would provide another man for you. Someone you could give your love to and who would love you back." She turned to face Margaret. "And when you found Thomas...I just knew he was the one God provided for you."

"But, Mama, why would God send a Yankee after all I've been through and when He knows I've always hated them?"

"God has His ways of teaching us in our weakness. You don't feel that hatred in your heart anymore, do you?"

"No, ma'am." Margaret couldn't help the wondering tone of her voice. The hate was gone. "It's strange, but I don't. I hated everyone and everything in the North, and now I'm falling in love with a Yankee. God really does work in mysterious ways, doesn't He, Mama?"

"Yes, yes, He does." Mama cranked the mill. "Enough talk about Thomas. We need to think about getting supper on. Papa took a pot of fish stew over to the fort. He should be back soon."

"Yes, ma'am." Margaret stood and pulled back the curtain, glancing out to catch a glimpse of Thomas. *Lord, did You really send Thomas like Mama said?*

June was talking to Thomas.

June Marie...there you go...pestering Thomas, just like

I told you not to!

"Mama, June is out there with Thomas. Should she come back in the house and let him finish his work?"

"Just as soon as I put the coffee on, pull the cornbread out of the oven, and reheat the stew."

"I'll go get her then." Margaret started for the door.

Jeremiah awakened from his nap and started to cry.

"Don't worry, Mama. I'll get him."

"Thank you, dear."

"Sissy's coming, Jeremiah."

12

Thomas found great joy in pulling the weeds around Mr. Logan's Brussels sprouts. The physical task caused him pain, but the pleasure came from the normalcy of the chore. The earth in his hands and the smell of the fresh vegetables exhilarated him. These simple tasks differed so much from his time aboard ship. His job there was to intercept blockade runners and, if necessary, fire on his fellow man.

June skipped through the rows of the fall garden.

"Hello, June. What brings ye to the garden this fine day?"

"Hello, Mr. Murphy. I'm keeping me busy since Mama and Margaret have some talking to do." June stuffed the remnants of a biscuit into her mouth.

"You've got a bit of honey right here on yer mouth." Thomas pointed at his lips.

June licked the spot and wiped her mouth on her sleeve. "Is it gone now?"

"Ye did a good job, lass. Good thing yer papa has those honeybees or else you'd be eatin' dry biscuits."

"Eww, I don't want no dry biscuits!"

"Well, ye must have done a mighty good deed to deserve one of yer mama's delicious biscuits this soon before suppertime."

June pushed some soil around with her toe. "Oh, I

don't know. I s'pose you might say I'm one of Mama's favorites."

"Of course ye are." He chuckled and leaned close. "Can I tell ye a wee secret, lass?"

"Sure, I like secrets."

He looked from side to side, pretending to make sure no one was listening. "Ye happen to be one of my favorites as well."

"I already knew that." She plucked off a leaf and used it to point at Thomas. "I heard a secret about you too."

Thomas perked up at this revelation. "Did ye now? And just what sort of secret have ye heard about me, lass?"

She used her leaf to touch Thomas on the chest with each word. "I heard you're in love with Margaret."

Thomas hid his surprise. "Now where did ye hear such a thing as that?" *Have I been so obvious in my feelings?*

"Why, Lizbeth told me, of course. She said that since you don't have feelings for her, you're obviously in love with Margaret."

Relief washed over Thomas that it wasn't his actions that caused her assumptions.

"Besides, anyone could tell you got feelings for Margaret by the way you act when you're around her. I saw you lookin' at her at the dinner table and how you couldn't even talk when she asked if you would pass the mashed taters." June mocked Thomas. "'I...I...I certainly can, lass.'" Then she giggled, causing red curls to bounce around her head.

He *had* let his feelings show. He'd have to be more careful. He couldn't get thrown out. If that happened...Margaret would never know how desperate he was for her to return the feelings he was harboring deep inside.

June giggled.

Thomas decided to turn the tables on her. "Here I am working in the garden, minding my own business, when ye come out here and tell me there are rumors afoot concerning me. Now what would yer mama think if she found out yer spreading gossip right here in front of the Brussels sprouts?"

"You ain't gonna tell Mama none of what I said, are you, Mr. Murphy?" June was anxious.

"I suppose I might be persuaded to keep my mouth shut."

"How?"

"How about if ye keep quiet about what ye hear about me, and I'll do the same for you." Thomas stuck his hand out. "Is it a deal?"

"It's a deal." She let go of his hand. "Mr. Murphy, if you court Margaret, you better tell Papa. Mama says that's what boys do here in the South."

"I'll take that into consideration, lass. But don't ye think I might ought to ask Miss Margaret's permission first?"

"That might be a good idea."

The sound of gunfire cracked in the distance.

Heavy steps came running up the property line.

Thomas grabbed June and pushed her behind him.

Mr. Logan ran around the shed and toward the house. Plumes of dust exploded from the dry ground with every step. "Thomas, take June and get in the house as quick as you can."

"Aye, sir, but what on earth has ye so worked up?"

"It's a raid. I saw a boatload of Union soldiers come ashore—they're coming up the beach. Now grab the goat and take my daughter in the house while I gather some supplies!"

Thomas didn't question why Mr. Logan would want a goat inside the house. He ran to the pen, threw the lead rope around the animal's neck, swept June up, and went inside the house.

Margaret sat in the front room, holding Jeremiah in her lap, rocking back and forth in the chair, as tranquil as can be.

"Mama, Mama, it's a raid." June jumped out of his arms and ran to the kitchen.

~*~

"Are they coming this way?" Margaret sat up straight and stopped rocking, fear making her voice wobble and her heart pound.

Jeremiah stiffened, then settled back into sleep.

"I'm afraid so, lass. Tell me what needs to be done."

She hurried to Mama and Papa's room to lay Jeremiah down and returned.

Thomas was still holding on to Nanny Sue's lead rope.

"Quick, bring the goat. We'll all hide in the pantry once they come onto our property."

Thomas followed her, tugging the protesting goat along behind him.

Mama was gathering up anything of value and hauling it into the pantry with tears streaming down her face. She stopped, her gaze going blank, a hand rubbing her forehead.

"Thomas, take Nanny Sue to the pantry and tie her to the hook on the back wall. Then go help Papa with what he needs. On your way back, snatch up some grass to keep Nanny Sue busy. June, run into Mama's room and gather up a few toys for Jeremiah...we're gonna need them when he wakes up." Margaret hurried everyone along, aware that her mother was too stunned to think. "Mama, go get Jeremiah, and gather up whatever he'll need to stay in the pantry."

Mama didn't move. "I've got to get everything of value into the pantry or else they'll steal what little we have left."

Margaret put her hands on her shoulders. "Mama, listen to me. We got through this before and this time we're prepared for them. Now go...get Jeremiah."

Her mother nodded, wiped her eyes, and went to their room.

Papa came into the house with his arms full of farming supplies. He dumped the load into Thomas's arms. "Here, take these tools into the pantry." Papa looked at Margaret. His gaze swept around the room. "They're coming up over the dunes. Everything stored away?"

"Yes, sir, as far as I can tell. What about Celia?"

"She'll have to fend for herself. Can't rightly bring a donkey into the house."

"Can you think of anything else we'll need, Papa?"

"Just one more thing."

Papa left the room and returned with his rifle and powder flask. "All right, I want everyone in the pantry...now!"

Thomas stood at the door of the pantry and helped everyone inside.

"Papa, wait. Elizabeth's not here." Margaret gasped, her hand on the doorframe.

"Oh, Lord, help us," Mama cried from inside the pantry.

Papa's expression broke, as if his heart had melted inside. "She's down at the Langley place again."

"You have to go get her, Jebediah." Mama's cries filled the pantry.

Papa ran to the kitchen door. "I don't see her coming up from the bay."

Thomas took a look out the front window. "She's not coming from this way either, but the soldiers are up to the property line." He went and stood beside Papa. "I'll go and fetch her for ye, Mr. Logan."

"No," Margaret screamed. "You can't go out there. If the soldiers don't kill you, the neighbors will."

Thomas turned to her.

Their gazes locked.

She must have looked like a crazed woman.

But in his eyes, she only saw love.

"She's right, Thomas. You can't go out there, and I'm not leaving this family. If she stays at Langley's place, she'll be fine. The old man has an arsenal of weapons at hand. We'll have to deal with Elizabeth when this is over. Now everyone get in the pantry."

Margaret moved to the back of the room and sat down on the wood floor. June stood trembling in the middle of the pantry. Margaret held her hands out. The little girl crawled into her lap and buried her face against her chest.

After the last raid, Papa had knocked out the wall between the pantry and the linen closet. There was so much more room now.

"Give me a hand, Thomas."

He pressed the sheet of wood against the door. Papa pulled a nail from his pocket and hammered it into the wall in case the lock didn't hold. He drove a nail into each side of the wood. "I've got it from here. Go see to the women."

"Mrs. Logan, are ye all right back there?"

She closed her eyes and nodded, clutching her baby.

Thomas sat down beside Margaret and June. He pulled her head to his shoulder. "Everything will be all right, lass."

Margaret whispered to Thomas, "What if they find Elizabeth? What if they…?"

"She's in the Lord's hands now. Let's pray for her."

Thomas offered his hand and Margaret took it into hers. "I can't pray." She tried but couldn't get the words out. "Will you?"

"Of course I will."

While Thomas prayed a great and mighty hedge of protection over the family and also for Elizabeth's safety, Papa drove nail after nail into the wood.

Margaret held tight to Thomas's strong hand, tears wetting her face as she stifled the desperate sobs. Even with Union soldiers invading their land, she felt safe inside the pantry with Thomas next to her. But an ache in her heart reminded her of one of the parables she'd learned as a child. *Please, Lord Jesus, find Your lost sheep.*

13

It was all she and Mama could do to keep everyone quiet when the small space included a baby, one rambunctious little girl, and a nanny goat. Margaret wasn't sure what was worse, the lack of fresh air or the strong smell of a goat and six sweaty bodies inside the tiny room.

Screams pierced the air outside, echoing through the pantry.

Everyone froze, silence filling the small room.

"Papa, we have to go out there. The Yankees have Elizabeth!" She buried her face in Thomas's sleeve and sobbed. "She doesn't sound right at all, Thomas. I know they're doing something terrible to her."

Papa waved a hand toward Margaret. "Hush up! It doesn't sound right because it's not Elizabeth. Now listen close!"

Thomas cupped his hand and whispered into Margaret's ear. "He's right, lass. Listen. Those are men screaming."

"How can you tell it's men? It sounds like a bunch of schoolgirls." Margaret tried to whisper, but the words came out loud. "What's happening out there?"

As quickly as the screaming started…it stopped.

~*~

No more sounds came from beyond the pantry.

It seemed as if an hour passed before Papa finally gave the word he was ready to open the door.

"Thomas, would you hand me the hammer there beside you?" Papa asked.

Thomas picked up the hammer and stood. "Don't ye fret, sir. I'll remove those nails for ye."

"All right then, I believe I'll let you." Papa moved out of Thomas's way.

The soldiers hadn't come into the house.

But Elizabeth was still somewhere out there.

Thomas helped Margaret up from the floor as Papa pushed the pantry door open.

When the door opened, June bolted from the pantry like a wild animal released from its cage.

"June Marie Logan, get back in here now." Terror sounded in Mama's voice. Mama didn't usually show fearfulness around the smaller children.

"It's OK. It's all clear outside." June stuck her nose in the air and sniffed extra loud. "Papa, I smell something burning!"

Papa took Jeremiah and helped Mama up off the floor. "All right now, June, come back in here and gather up Jeremiah's toys. You need to watch over him for a while."

Margaret stood in the kitchen, which appeared to be intact.

As June danced back toward them, she suddenly screamed and grabbed her arm. Margaret and Thomas ran to her. Mama and Papa were right behind them.

"What's the matter?" Margaret asked as she knelt.

June lifted her arm. A bee's stinger was embedded in her flesh. "Something bited me!" June exclaimed. Her arm was swelling even as she cried.

The dying honeybee twitched on the floor. Margaret mashed it with her foot.

Mama took June's hand, picked up Jeremiah, and disappeared into her and Papa's bedroom.

Papa wasted no time. "Thomas, help me close all the windows. Margaret, get some towels and stuff them under the doors. I know what those Yankees were screaming about. They tried to steal the hives and the bees are swarming!"

Thomas jumped to action.

Margaret followed suit, jamming towels under the thresholds of both doors. "Papa, it looks like the smoke from whatever they set on fire has the bees herded into one area at the west side of the yard," Margaret called as she surveyed the back of the property.

"You're right. I don't think I'll even need the smoker." He abandoned his preparation of the smoker and rubbed his chin. "OK, then…Thomas, gather up those garden tools and drag them back out to the shed. When you're done, meet me out back. I need your help to find the queen and get her back into the hive. When she's in place, the swarm should return."

"But, sir, how will we ever find one particular bee in that giant swarm?"

"It's not as hard as you think. One of her wings is clipped." He gave Thomas a sideways grin. "She don't fly so good."

Thomas raised his eyebrows and wasted no time getting the tools.

Papa turned his attention to Margaret. "All right, I want you to unhitch Nanny Sue and take her back out to her pen. As soon as we get the queen back in the hive, you and Thomas can survey the damage outside. And for heaven's sake, see what those Yankees set on fire."

"Yes, sir," Margaret answered.

Papa opened his bedroom door a crack.

Mama was sitting on the bed, doctoring June's bee sting.

"Caroline, when I get the queen bee back inside the hive, you and I will make sure that Yankee vessel is gone, and then we'll go find our daughter."

Tears slipped down Mama's cheeks as she nodded.

The dread Margaret had kept at bay returned with a vengeance.

~*~

"Why would they burn our cotton?"

Thomas heard the anguish in Margaret's voice as he doused the charred cotton with water. "I don't know, lass. It's quite valuable up north. They could have sold it for much more than it's worth...even used it for bandages."

"They burned it out of pure meanness." Margaret tramped around beside the garden, kicking a rock. "We won't have any money to trade with. And just look at the garden, they took everything!"

"That's not true, lass. They didn't take those green ones over there. What's yer papa call them, collard greens?"

Margaret managed a snicker at his mangled pronunciation.

"All right now, there ye go makin' fun of the way I speak." He smiled at her. "And look, they didn't take the time to dig up those potatoes, and those plants over there growing up the fence line."

"Stupid Yankees probably don't even know what black-eyed peas are."

Thomas scrubbed though his scraggly beard, trying to avoid the fact that he'd never heard of anything called black-eyed peas either. "Come on, lass, let's walk around the property and see if anything else has been bothered."

"At least they didn't break into Papa's shed." Margaret ran her fingers across the locked shed door as she walked around the corner. They reached Celia's pen next to the shed, and she froze. "Oh no, they took our donkey too."

Thomas put his arms around Margaret. She turned into his embrace and cried on his shoulder. He patted her back. "I'm so sorry, lass."

"First they burn our cotton, then they steal our food, and now they took Celia. You don't think they're planning to eat her, do you, Thomas?"

"No, lass, I don't think so. I'm sure they used her to pack off all the food they gathered."

"And…who knows…what's happened…to Elizabeth."

"Hush, child, yer mama and papa will bring her home directly. Everything will be all right." Thomas tried his best to console her.

She pulled away. "How do you know, Thomas? Has anything good ever come out of this horrible war?"

He gazed into violet eyes that seemed to have no end. Despite the tear-stained cheeks, red nose, and the dust that had collected in her hair during their pantry stay, Margaret Logan was more beautiful than ever. "Come, let's have a walk."

~*~

Thomas sat down and patted the dried wood as an invitation for Margaret to join him. She sat, probably closer to him than was proper, but those blue eyes of his could be quite a distraction. "Thomas, I want to thank you for comforting me through so many of the trials we've been through lately. I've always thought of myself as the strong one, but lately it seems I'm going to pieces over everything."

"Ye don't have to thank me, lass, and believe me, yer a very strong lady. The way you took charge of the house when those soldiers were approaching was a thing to behold. I certainly didn't know what to do until ye set me to task."

"Yes, you did seem a bit at a loss at the time." She giggled just a little.

"All right now, don't ye go teasing me again."

Margaret cleared her throat. "Well, unfortunately, that wasn't our first raid."

"Oh?"

"Yes, the first time was even worse. They came inside the house." She looked down at her left hand. "They stole the ring my fiancé gave me. Broke my heart."

Thomas touched her hand. "I'm sorry, lass. Now I understand how you knew exactly what to do."

"Thomas, I want to thank you for not pulling away when I held on to you in the pantry and at the donkey pen. I don't know what came over me." Margaret was still uneasy. She glanced around, hoping none of the Yankees hid from them. "It's just that Celia came all the way from New Orleans with us. I remember one time when June was picking primrose...we call them buttercups down here...anyway, June pressed the flowers into Celia's face and covered her entire nose with yellow powder. Well, that donkey huffed and puffed and let out the biggest sneeze you've ever heard. June had to run to the washtub after that."

Thomas laughed with her. He straddled the old log and held his hands out to her.

Margaret accepted his hands and felt her cheeks blossom with heat.

"Miss Margaret, I can't hold this in any longer. I need to tell ye that I've had feelings for ye since I first laid eyes on ye that day at the bay. Ye say that nothing good has ever come out of this war, but I think that you—finding me—was the best thing that ever could have happened. I've been waiting for the opportunity to see if it would be all right if I asked yer papa if I might court ye." His cheeks were a bit flushed as he looked away. "Now I understand if the answer is no. I know how ye feel about Yankees, but in actuality I'm much more of an Irishman than a Yankee."

"Thomas, I'm not going to lie and say I haven't had feelings for you too. I realize now that the circumstances we are in can't be blamed on one person...especially not you." She looked down at their hands. He'd become stronger since that day she'd found him. She lifted one of his hands to her heart. "I suppose I'm willing to open my heart again."

"Oh, lass, I'm so happy to hear it." Thomas wrapped both arms around her for a moment and then took her hand again. "I plan to ask yer papa's permission as soon as I can."

Margaret stared out at the water.

"What is it, Margaret?"

"I can't help but think you'll be strong enough to

return to the North soon. Then what will become of us?"

"It's true. I will have to eventually return and reconnect with my unit. And I'm needing to check on my father and brothers. But I promise ye...wherever I go...no matter how far...I'll always come back to ye."

"I believe you." She closed her eyes when Thomas gently squeezed her hand.

They walked back toward the house.

In the distance, Mama and Papa's voices were raised, as if they were arguing. Apparently, they'd found Elizabeth, because her sister was shrieking about something at the top of her lungs.

14

"Right this way, miss." Thomas struggled to pull the wooden chair out, offering Margaret a seat. The task would have been much easier had he not been wearing Mr. Logan's dress coat that was two sizes too small. Every move seemed impossible.

"Why, thank you, sir." She put a gloved hand to her mouth as she giggled.

Thomas took a seat in the chair across from her. He reached across the small card table for her hand and made a grunting sound when the coat wouldn't allow him to extend his arm fully. "I'm sorry, lass, but this coat has got to go."

"I understand completely. Papa is a might bit smaller than you, Thomas."

"Aye, that he is, lass." He sat back down. The sweet fragrance of the rose water she wore wafted in the air, even with the table of food before them. The soft candlelight made her eyes sparkle like a beautiful full moon rising over the bay.

"And might I say that ye look lovelier than ever this evening."

Her raven hair glistened with every movement of her head. There was something about this woman that made him want to forsake everything and be with her the rest of his life.

"Thank you, Thomas." A smile appeared. "I wasn't sure I'd like you clean-shaven, but I must admit you're even more handsome than before."

"I'm glad ye like it, but it wasn't easy taking a razor to my jaw after all this time." He held his hand out.

She accepted it and bowed her head.

"Father, we come to Ye this evening and ask a blessing on this meal and on the hands of the ones who prepared it. I thank Ye, Father, for bringing me to this wonderful home and to these fine people who love Ye with all their hearts. Thank Ye for Mr. and Mrs. Logan, who care enough to allow this special time for Margaret and myself since we're not in a situation where I can court her properly. I pray, Father, that Ye would heal those who have been injured in this horrible war and that it will all be over within short order. In Yer Son's name I pray. Amen."

"Thank you, Thomas. That was beautiful."

"Yer welcome. Can I serve ye, miss?"

"Yes, please."

Thomas began serving the food. Even though the fare was meager, the taste would be delicious since Mrs. Logan had cooked it. "I still can't believe yer mama would go to all this trouble so we can have some sort of courtship. Ye have a mighty fine mama, Margaret Logan."

"I have a feeling she likes you, Thomas. You've done so much for us since you've been here."

"Well, I've been here so long, I'm lucky she's not ready to throw me out like old fish."

"Don't be ridiculous. Besides, I happen to know that her daughter cares a great deal for you too."

"Is that so?" He handed her plate back. "Well,

truth be known, I happen to feel mighty attached to that daughter of hers. Fine-looking woman, she is."

A blush rose in Margaret's cheeks.

They ate their candlelight dinner in silence, sharing an occasional flirting glance. Love was growing; his heart belonged to her.

Margaret took a sip of water. She looked away from the table; her silhouette glowed against the candlelight. "Thomas."

"Yes, my lass."

"I have to ask…when do you plan to go back up north?"

Why would she bring up that sad subject?

"I fear that I probably need to leave right after Christmas." His heart, so joyful before, melted toward a deep well of dread.

"Oh, Thomas, we'll have the most wonderful Christmas ever." She spoke as if she'd not asked the question that would tear them apart. "Of course, we won't have very much food after those Yankees raided our garden. But Mama can make a feast out of nothing. I can hardly wait."

Thomas heard the pain in her voice. "Aye, lass, if only I could, I would take ye to the finest restaurants in all the land."

"And I would love to take my place amongst all the fine ladies." She faked an accent as she spoke.

Thomas stood, bowed, and offered his hand to her. "May I have this dance, my lady?"

"Why, of course you may."

There wasn't the beauty of a bow sliding across a well-tuned violin. There was no gentle strumming of a harp playing softly in the background. There wasn't even the warm melody of piano chords, and yet they danced around the candlelit room. Their music was the beating of two longing hearts coming together...forever...entwined as one.

"May I kiss ye, my love?"

Her eyes closed and her face turned up. "Oh, yes...yes."

Their lips came together in an embrace as soft and gentle as a warm summer breeze.

15

Margaret swiped loose strands of hair from her face. "Bet you never thought you'd be doing this, did you, Papa?" She reached inside the trap with a stick and coaxed out a big blue crab.

"Well, I don't know about that. I've had quite a few jobs in my lifetime, but I can't say I've ever had opportunity to boil crabs before. Now crawfish are a whole different story."

The crab opened its claws, ready to attack. She pushed him over to Papa who quickly grabbed him by his back legs and dumped him into the pot of boiling water.

Margaret winced. "Seems so cruel."

"You won't be saying that once you've had a taste of him."

"Ugh, I don't know if I'll be able to eat something I've watched boil to death."

"That's why June is in the house. She'd be awful upset to know what we're doing out here. Now start pulling out the rest of those crabs. Your mama's gonna think we're foolin' around instead of doing our job."

"Yes, sir."

Thomas was working in the garden.

"Hey, Thomas," Papa yelled over his shoulder. "Would you mind gathering up some more wood for me? I need to keep this water boiling."

"Aye, sir. I've seen a good bit of palm out by the slough. I'll fetch it for ye."

Papa stirred the pot before reaching for another crab. "That's a good man, Margaret."

"Yes, he is."

"Papa, I'm worried about Elizabeth. She's acting so strange lately."

Papa rubbed his forehead with the back of his hand. Margaret knew he was probably having a hard time with the answer. "I have a feeling Elizabeth is jealous of you and Thomas. Why don't you try talking with her about it?"

"I have. She won't listen."

"I know what you mean. Honestly, I'm worried about Elizabeth myself. She's starting to act just like my cousin Emma."

Margaret squinted in the bright afternoon sun. *There's that name again.* "Who's Cousin Emma?"

He picked up the crabs as Margaret pushed them toward him and sent them down into the boiling water. "Well, I had a cousin back in Louisiana. First child of my Aunt Joan and Uncle Lucas. We were about the same age and all of us cousins grew up together." Papa's gaze took on a faraway look. "Anyway, by the time Emma and I were around thirteen, fourteen, she...changed. Everyone in the family knew she wasn't right, but no one knew what to do for her."

"What do you mean she wasn't right?"

The last crab ran out of the trap and tried to make his escape by walking sideways across the plank the crab trap rested on. He ended up falling off upside down on the ground, his limbs flailing about wildly. Margaret raised her eyebrows and shook her head.

"I'm not picking that up, Papa."

He chuckled and bent over and picked up the stray crab, plopping him headlong into the bubbling abyss. He then took the long-handled, slotted spoon from the pot and tapped it on the side, shaking off the water.

"Well, some days she seemed as happy as could be...too happy even."

"Now how can someone be too happy?"

"Well, you have your happy and then you have your—too happy."

Margaret rolled her eyes. "Be serious, Papa."

"All right, all right. Emma would have spells where she'd dance and sing and carry on, even in the middle of the night. Aunt Joan had to watch her when she was like that or she might just give away everything they had."

"I don't know, Papa. Dancing and being generous doesn't sound all that bad to me."

"No, but then there'd be times when she would get so low and blue, it seemed she might not come out of it." Papa stuck the spoon back into the boiling water and gave the water a swirl. "Those were the real bad times. When she got like that, her ma and pa would lock her away so she wouldn't hurt herself." He set the spoon down on the wooden plank and looked away. "That's my real fear...that Elizabeth will become like Emma."

The air seemed to become as thick as molasses.

Thomas came up behind them, his arms loaded with palm fronds.

Margaret was glad for the interruption since she wasn't sure she could speak.

"Here ye go, Mr. Logan." He set the foliage on the

ground next to the fire.

"Thank you, Thomas. You're a good man."

"Aye, yer welcome. Anything else I can do for ye?" His words were aimed at Papa, but his eyes were trained on Margaret.

"Keep working up an appetite. We've got a lot of crab to eat here." Papa stoked the fire with the palm branches.

Thomas laughed. He gave Margaret a quick wink before turning around.

Papa lifted one of the crabs with the spoon and examined it. "Almost done." He dropped it back in the pot and stirred it around. "Margaret, I don't want to continue this conversation about Emma. It doesn't have a happy ending."

She wiped her hands on a rag. "I understand." She picked up Mama's big bowl and held it for him. She knew she needed to say something reassuring. "Papa, I'm sure Elizabeth isn't going to turn out like your cousin Emma. Maybe this will pass soon."

"I sure hope you're right, honey."

Margaret hoped so too.

~*~

Margaret carried the heavy bowl of steaming crabs to the porch.

Papa put out the fire and followed after her.

The seafood feast smelled wonderful, even if it did look gruesome.

Mama had set out a clean bowl, two nutcrackers, and a few other kitchen tools to help with the job of cleaning the crabs.

Papa made easy work of removing the claws and

legs for later. He handed Margaret the warm orange-red bodies, and she began peeling everything that wasn't sweet, white meat. Even though she loved the flavor of fresh crabmeat, she most likely wouldn't eat much. The process of cleaning the creatures' entrails always turned her stomach.

Papa, on the other hand, ate more than his share of the crabs while he helped clean them. He slid a piece of claw cartilage out of his mouth, removing the meat that had been attached to it. "Praise the Lord for these crabs," he said with his mouth full.

Margaret picked meat out and let it land in the bowl sitting in her lap. "Yes, sir, we sure are blessed to have them, especially after we gave so much food away to the neighbors after the raid."

"We won't be having any more eggs for a while, that's for sure." He sat back in his chair.

"I don't think June has yet forgiven those Union soldiers for taking Mr. Milton's chickens."

They both laughed.

"She does love her eggs." Papa began to rock his chair. "At least they were able to save a few…should have chickens again real soon."

"At least we still have milk, thanks to Nanny Sue."

"Yes, but that won't last long if we don't get her bred. I need to find out if Old Man Goodman lost his buck in the raid."

Margaret's eyebrows hiked up. "I sure hope not. We can barely do without eggs. Milk is another thing altogether."

"I know, I know." Papa retrieved his pipe from the windowsill and tamped on the barrel. "I heard some talk down at the port that Mr. Lincoln was re-elected to another term. Maybe he'll finally do something to end this war and things can get back to the way they used to be." Papa sat up straight.

"What is it, Papa?"

"I saw a ship's spire over the dunes...probably another blockade runner heading into Galveston." Papa relaxed. He picked up a crab claw and pulled out a fat piece of meat. "Rumor has it Galveston's the only accessible Confederate port since Mobile Bay was captured back in August. Thank heavens, Texas gets first shot at anything and everything the ships bring in from Havana." He popped the meat into his mouth.

"Too bad for the men on those ships that so many people on Galveston Island are ill with yellow fever."

"Yep, thank the Lord it hasn't come over to the peninsula...yet." He picked up another claw and a long, thin pick to dig more meat. "I tell you what, those blockade runners are really something..." Papa droned on, but Margaret wasn't paying attention. Her time with Thomas was growing short, and she wanted something to make their last few weeks memorable.

"Margaret, you haven't heard a word I've said."

"What, Papa?"

"And you've put some shells in the meat bowl and meat in the shell bowl, for heaven's sake. What's going on in that mind of yours, girl?"

"Oh, Papa, I'm sorry." She picked pieces of crab shell out of the fresh meat she'd taken so much time to clean. "I've been thinking about Thomas."

"Yeah, I had a feeling that might be the case. I suppose with Christmas just around the corner, he's leaving soon."

"I can hardly bear to think about it."

"Look at me, Margaret."

She turned.

"Thomas has asked my permission to marry you."

She gasped. Her heart skipped a beat. "And what did you say?"

"I told him I'd think about it." He folded his hands. "So...how do you feel about marrying a Yankee?"

Margaret looked deep into her papa's eyes. "I don't care what he is, Papa. I love him."

"I had a feeling you might say that. I suppose I'll tell him I give my blessing."

She leaned over and threw her arms around his neck. "Oh, thank you, Papa. Thank you."

Movement in the tall grass startled Margaret. "Look, Papa!"

Celia, their donkey, was moving through the tall grass.

Margaret's excitement about Thomas's imminent proposal spilled over to her feelings about Celia's return. She ran to the bedraggled animal and gave her a big hug. "Oh, Celia, I've never been so happy to see a donkey in my whole life."

Papa was laughing. "Margaret, I didn't know you cared so much."

"Oh, Papa."

16

Margaret planned to enjoy her last few weeks with Thomas.

She gathered everyone into the kitchen.

Mama shifted Jeremiah to her other leg. "All right now, you've got us all in here. What on earth is so important?"

"I'm sorry, but I've been waiting all morning for Thomas to go outside with Papa before I could tell you all my idea."

June tapped her fingers on the table and rolled her eyes up at the ceiling. "Come on, Margaret, I got stuff I need to be doing."

"Oh, hush up, June Marie. You no more have anything to do than Jeremiah does."

"Humph, I do so!"

"June." Mama put an end to what was sure to be a battle of words. "Go on, Margaret, tell us your idea."

"All right, I've come up with an idea to make Thomas's last few weeks with us a special time for everyone." She paused for responses. When none came, she continued. "In honor of Thomas's deceased mama and sister, God rest their souls, I think our family should celebrate Advent this Christmas."

She looked at their faces, hoping for looks of excitement, anticipation, anything, but she only saw blank stares. "Well, doesn't that sound like fun?"

"What the heck is Advent?" June spit the words out as though Margaret had suggested they eat worms. "'Cause I ain't giving up Christmas for no Advent, that's for sure."

"Hush up, June," Mama intervened. "I've heard of Advent, but it's not something we ever celebrated. So I don't know much about it. But…we'd all be happy to hear what it's all about. Right, girls?"

June responded with another harrumph. Elizabeth, on the other hand, remained silent.

"Thank you, Mama." She pulled a piece of paper from her apron pocket and unfolded it. "Thomas told me everything he knows about Advent and I wrote it all down." She smoothed out the paper on the table where they all could see. "Here is a drawing I made of how I think everything should be arranged. I'm sorry I can't sketch very well, but you get the idea. This circle is like a wreath. It should probably be made from pine boughs. Now I know we don't have much pine here on the peninsula, but we have plenty of other foliage that should work just as well."

Mama raised her hand and stopped her. "Why don't you tell us what the celebration is for? I mean, what's the purpose of it?"

Margaret slowed down and thought a moment. "Well…the way I understand it, it's a way to prepare for Jesus's second coming while we remember His first coming in the manger in Bethlehem."

"All right, I can't say that I understand the purpose for it, but at least it doesn't go against anything we believe in. So go on."

June leaned across the table and pointed at Margaret's drawing. "What's that supposed to be?"

"Those are candles. Can't you tell by the flame at

the top?" Margaret replied.

Miss Priss scrunched up her lips, tilted her head, and squinted at the paper. "Not really. You sure aren't a very good draw-er, Margaret."

"June Marie..." Mama called her full name again. "Now that's enough."

"Yes, ma'am."

Margaret continued, trying to rekindle the enthusiasm she'd felt when she started the conversation. "OK, Advent starts on the fourth Sunday before Christmas. That means we need to have the first one on November twenty-seventh, and that's right around the corner. The first candle here stands for hope." She paused to look at her notes. "It's a whole week for everyone to think about and remember the prophets in the Bible who foretold Jesus's first coming."

June leaned over, peering deep into the drawing. "Which one is the second candle, this one or this one over here?" June pointed as she asked.

"It's this one. The second candle stands for love. It is a remembrance of Bethlehem and how God showed His love for us by sending Jesus."

June leaned back over Margaret's drawing. "So this must be the third candle, right?"

Margaret smiled. "Good guess, but no, it's this one. The third candle is all about joy and the shepherds who were the first people to ever hear about Jesus being born in Bethlehem."

June pointed to the candle at the center of the wreath. "Well, then this has to be the fourth candle."

"No, silly, it's this one."

"I know, but I got every other guess wrong. Thought I might as well get this one wrong too."

Everyone laughed at what June said, except Elizabeth, that is. She sat on her chair with a face as hard as stone and arms folded across her chest.

Margaret was encouraged that at least Mama and June were becoming interested. "OK, the fourth candle stands for peace. And Lord knows, we could use some peace on earth right about now. Anyway, it's when we remember the angels that told about Christ's birth. Then, of course, we have the biggest candle here in the center of the wreath." She smiled at June. "We burn it on Christmas Eve in honor of Jesus and His death on the cross. And that's it." She sat down at the table and looked at her mama and sisters, waiting for any questions.

Mama bent down and picked up the carved duck toy from the floor and handed it to Jeremiah. "So is that all there is to it, lighting candles?"

Margaret perked up and shook her head. She held up her notes to them. "Oh, no, there's scripture reading and singing, and I thought we could make special meals to go along with the celebration."

Mama furrowed her brow and adjusted Jeremiah on her lap again. "Margaret, you know we don't have much in the line of food to cook for a celebration."

"I know, Mama, but we're gonna eat something anyhow, so we might as well make a celebration out of it." She pleaded with her eyes, knowing what a soft spot Mama had for the Christmas season. "Come on, Mama, can we please do this? Besides, it's not the food that matters. It's that we remember Jesus on His birthday."

Mama sighed. "All right, Margaret, we'll do this, but it will take some work to make it happen."

Margaret threw her arms around her mother and

Jeremiah. "Oh, thank you, thank you, Mama. This is going to be the best Christmas we've ever had."

Mama started giggling along with Jeremiah and then June. "Margaret, you're going to squeeze the life out of us, for heaven's sake."

June joined them on the other side of the table. "Mama, can I start collecting the stuff to make the Advent wreath?"

Mama arose from her chair. "Yes, yes, but don't stray too far from the house."

June smiled and jumped up and down. "I won't." She grabbed her baby brother's feet. "We're gonna have an Advent, Jeremiah!" He kicked his feet and giggled.

Margaret tapped her finger on her temple. "OK, I'm gonna need to find five candles. Mama, how many beeswax candles do we have in the pantry?"

"I don't know. You'll have to check for yourself," Mama answered.

Elizabeth got up and headed for the kitchen door.

"Elizabeth," Mama called to her. "I need you to give me a hand with Jeremiah while I cook.

"Elizabeth, did you hear me?"

Elizabeth opened the door without turning around. "I'm going to Mr. Langley's house to help him with his son. He needs me."

"Elizabeth," Mama called.

The door slammed behind her.

"Just let her go, Mama. I've got Jeremiah."

"What is wrong with Lizbeth? I guess she don't even care about the Baby Jesus!" June shook her head in dismay.

"Come on, June, we'll take Jeremiah and go look for the Advent decorations together. Sound like fun?"

"Yeah, at least some of us love Baby Jesus."

Mama smiled at her youngest daughter through glistening eyes.

But inside, Margaret was certain her mama's heart was breaking to pieces for Elizabeth.

17

Thomas's hand brushed against Margaret's as they walked the property in search of the perfect tree for their Christmas celebration. She turned her hand and he took hold of it.

Thin stalks of purple seagrass bowed their heads as the crisp late-November breeze whipped past.

"What exactly have ye got in mind for a Christmas tree, lass?"

"Oh, I don't know. I suppose anything we can find that the little ones can hang things on."

"Well, we've walked every inch of this property and haven't found anything yet."

"Oh!" Margaret stopped in her tracks.

"What is it, lass?"

"I just thought of something we could use. I know where there's a huge piece of coral that is sort of shaped like a tree. Of course, it won't have any foliage like a real tree, but we could add some palm fronds to it. That should work well enough, don't you think?"

"I suppose so. Where is it?"

"Over in the slough." Margaret pointed.

"Well, let's go and fetch it."

"Did you know Mama and Papa will celebrate twenty years of marriage next year?"

"Aye, twenty years, that's quite a legacy for you and yer sisters and brother. They're quite a good example for ye. And not much fighting between them either." He laughed.

"What, do Irish couples have a reputation of fighting?"

"It's not just the couples that like to fight. All good Irish like to fight."

Margaret swung their hands back and forth as they walked. She didn't look at him as she spoke. "Thomas...have you ever thought about...getting married?"

~*~

Her question caught him off-guard. Of course he'd thought about marriage. Of late he'd done a lot of thinking about marrying the raven-haired beauty. "Aye, I suppose I've always had a mind to get married and raise some children. And how about you, do ye ever think about marriage?" Thomas inwardly winced. *What are ye thinkin', ye fool? Of course she's thought about marriage. She was engaged, for heaven's sake.*

If he'd upset her, she didn't let it show. She did, however, stop swinging their hands and slowly rubbed his hand with her thumb. "Of course I have. It's every girl's dream to get married."

"I'm sure you're right about that. And what about children. Have ye ever thought about having children?"

A glow rose in her cheeks. "I suppose I'd like to have a child...or maybe two."

"Do ye now? Well then, lassie, you'd better find yerself a husband first."

Margaret softly tapped his arm.

Thomas burst out laughing. "Ye know, this

conversation reminds me of a tradition we had back in my homeland. Every year at Halloween time, it was a custom to prepare a dish called *cál ceannann*." He scratched his head. "I think here in America it's called colcannon. Anyway, it's a mixture of potatoes and cabbage or kale, boiled together with scallions."

They reached the log at the slough.

Margaret pointed to a mud bog. "There's the coral over there. Do you see it?"

"Aye, I do. Seems to be stuck in a bit of mud."

"Yes, it is." Margaret spoke in a more-than-nonchalant tone. "Looks like one of us will have to get wet and muddy."

"I suppose that would be me."

"Let's sit a spell before you go in after it."

"Sounds like a very good idea, lass."

They sat on the big log.

It was hard to believe that only a short time ago, she hated everything about him. His heart was ready to take the plunge. Now she was too.

"So I don't see how this cal...cal...whatever you call it, has anything to do with our conversation." Margaret drew him away from his thoughts.

"Oh, right, well, after the vegetables are mashed together with milk, butter, salt, and pepper, four little items would be stirred in, a thimble, a ring, a button, and a coin."

"Why would you do that?"

"The tradition says that each item has a meaning and whoever got one of them in their bowl, then that was a telling of their future."

"You don't really believe that, do you?"

"No, of course not, but I'm sure there are many who do."

"So tell me, what is the meaning of each thing?"

"Let's see, the coin meant you would have wealth. The ring meant that you would marry, and if you were already married, then your happiness would continue. Both the button and the thimble meant that the person would never marry."

"I suppose I'd need to find that ring now, wouldn't I?" She squeezed his arm.

"Aye, lass, I hope that ye would." Thomas began pulling off his boots and rolling up his trousers. "And I suppose I should go and fetch yer coral Christmas tree." He walked to the edge of the slough and stepped into the water before letting out a long, loud whistle. "Oh my, but this water is a might cold."

Margaret covered her mouth and giggled.

He would do anything for her, even wade through waist-deep, freezing-cold water to retrieve a piece of coral. If there had been any doubt before, there could be none after today. Thomas Murphy was madly in love.

~*~

Jeremiah toddled toward Thomas, his apple cheeks glowing and his hand outstretched. Thomas threaded a piece of string through a small hole in one of the seashells and tied it into a loop before the little boy reached him.

Margaret sat on the floor beside him, helping with the stringing. "Go on, ask him for more, Jeremiah."

Jeremiah tapped his palm. "Mo peas."

"Ye want another, do ye?"

Jeremiah nodded and took the seashell from Thomas's hand.

The huge piece of coral made a beautiful Christmas tree.

The two youngest children had done a good job decorating it with all sorts of offerings from the beach. Seashells, starfish, sand dollars, and even crab claws hung from bits of string.

Margaret cut red ribbons from an old skirt and added them here and there to give the makeshift tree a homey touch. It was a wonderful display of Christmas spirit, albeit a smelly one—thanks to the sea creatures.

Mr. Logan sat in his rocking chair, reading while they had their fun.

Mrs. Logan and Elizabeth were in the kitchen, preparing the evening meal, something they hadn't done together for some time.

Thomas felt a surge of happiness because of the wonderful family he'd come to know and love and that they allowed him to be a part of it.

"We did it, we did it. All the decorations are done!" June jumped up. "Come on, everybody! It's time for the Advent party to start!"

Mr. Logan must have dozed off in his chair, as June's outburst caused him to jump, sending his newspaper flying through the air.

Mrs. Logan called from the kitchen. "We'll be there in just a minute."

"Thomas, will you pull that table over here by my chair?" Mr. Logan sat up.

"Yes, sir, I'd be much obliged." Thomas moved the table already set up with a wreath and candles.

"Papa, Papa, can I light the first Advent candle, pleeeease?" June begged.

Mama entered the room.

Elizabeth trailed behind, her arms crossed, her

expression seeming to indicate a lack of desire to participate.

"Sure you can. Go fetch a stick from the fireplace," Papa answered June.

"Mr. Logan, wait. I was wondering if I might say something before we light the candle?" Thomas was solemn.

"Sure, son, go right ahead. Hold off a minute, June."

"Now, I've n'er done this before, so please allow me a bit o' grace."

~*~

"Don't worry, Thomas. You'll do just fine." Margaret patted his arm.

"My mam used to tell us that the first candle of Advent is for the prophet Isaiah, who foretold of the birth of Jesus." He looked over at Papa. "Might I borrow yer family Bible, Mr. Logan?"

"Of course you can. June, hop up and give Mr. Murphy the Bible."

"Yes, sir."

June had to use both hands to pick up the huge Bible. She took a long whiff of the leather binding before dropping the book into Thomas's hands.

"Ye think the leather smells nice, lass?" Thomas asked.

"Uh-huh," she answered before plopping back down.

Thomas thumbed to the book of Isaiah, chapter nine. He began to read. *"For unto us a Child is born, unto us a Son is given: and the government shall be upon His shoulder: and His name shall be called Wonderful,*

Counsellor, the mighty God, the everlasting Father, the Prince of Peace." He closed the Good Book and turned to Mr. Logan. "Would ye please say a prayer, sir?"

Papa cleared his throat. "Heavenly Father, we humble ourselves before Your throne. Lord, we thank You for those that have gone before us, our sweet baby Joseph and Thomas's mama and baby sister. Thank You, Father, for the time we had with them. And, Lord, we pray for Thomas's papa and brothers, that they would be safe and that this old war would be over soon. In Your Son's name we pray. Amen."

Thomas wiped away a tear after Papa's prayer.

Papa motioned to June. "Go on, you can light the candle now."

June set the small stick aflame.

Jeremiah stretched to see the candle being lit.

Thomas's face glowed with adoration as he watched the two little ones.

The candlelight flickering on their petite round faces was a beautiful sight.

Thomas reached for Margaret's hand and held it tight. Then he began to sing in a smooth tenor. *"Praise God from Whom all blessings flow."*

Margaret joined him in perfect harmony. *"Praise Him, all creatures here below."*

A loud crash made everyone stop singing.

Elizabeth stood. One of mama's good glasses lay shattered at her feet. She didn't move but stared blankly at the rest of the family. Then she turned and walked toward their bedroom.

Mrs. Logan buried her face in her hands.

"Come on now, let's sing." Papa said, lifting his mighty bass voice. *"Praise Him above, ye heavenly host. Praise Father, Son, and Holy Ghost. Amen."*

Margaret pulled a handkerchief from her sleeve and handed it to Mama. "She'll be all right, Mama. She's just got a case of the blues, that's all."

Mama leaned into Margaret's embrace. She spoke softly so the others wouldn't hear, but Thomas was so close he probably heard. Her words sounded heavy, desperate, hopeless. "She's not all right, Margaret, and she's not getting any better like we thought she would. She won't ever be all right again."

Could Mama be right? Was there no hope for poor Elizabeth? Her stomach tied itself in knots thinking about having to lock her away as they'd done to Papa's cousin Emma. But she couldn't think about it...not now with Thomas leaving in a few weeks. Margaret would do everything in her power to insure that her last days with Thomas would be a time they would remember...forever.

18

Margaret's legs seemed to turn to butter with every kiss Thomas placed on the back of her neck. Had they not been busy preparing a meal, she'd welcome his kisses. But there was cornbread to make and it wasn't getting done with all the tomfoolery going on. "Thomas Murphy, if you don't pay attention, you'll never learn how to make hot-water cornbread." She turned, smiled, and put her hand up to her neck where his lips had been.

"I'm sorry, lass, but I can't help myself." He kissed her forehead.

"Well, you need to behave." She wagged a finger at him.

"OK, OK, so why do ye call it hot-water cornbread? I've never heard of that before."

"Because, regular cornbread calls for eggs, and since there are no eggs on the entire peninsula, we have to make hot-water cornbread. It doesn't call for eggs."

"Aye, I see. And does it call for sugar?" He kissed the tip of her nose. "Because we have a fair amount of that, lass."

She shook her head at his silly pun, but couldn't help smiling. "Now stop it. We're ready to pour the boiling water over the cornmeal and lard. Measure out three quarters of a cup, and I'll add the salt."

Thomas poured the steaming hot liquid over the ingredients in the bowl. The lard melted into a puddle. "What shall I do now, mix it together?"

"Yes." She handed him a spatula. "It'll be sticky, but do your best to get it mixed."

A good amount of lard was being heated in the iron skillet. Margaret took the long-handled spoon from the spoon rest and stirred the big pot of black-eyed peas. She scooped out a small spoonful and set it to cool.

"Are ye hungry? Setting out a bit of those peas for yerself, are ye?"

"No, I need to have a taste to see if they're done."

"Well, go on then."

"I don't want to burn my mouth. They're boiling hot!"

"You've got a point there." He slapped the top of his cornbread dough ball with the spatula. "Seems to be well mixed, lass. What shall I do with it now?"

"You need to separate a small amount at a time and form it into cakes."

"Ye mean I have to put my hands into this sticky mess?"

"Aye, laddie, ye do." She giggled.

"So now yer going to mock the way I talk, are ye?" Thomas pulled the spatula out of the gooey mixture and poked it at her.

Margaret hopped around the kitchen. She couldn't remember when she'd laughed so hard.

Thomas backed her into the cabinets, taunting her.

"Don't you get that sticky thing on my clothes, Thomas Murphy. I don't want to have to change my dress."

"Well, fine then. I won't get it on yer dress."

Thomas touched the tip of her nose and lips. "Here, let me get that off ye." He wiped the spot of mixture on his trouser leg. "I think I missed a bit."

The kiss that followed caused Margaret's entire body to quiver. She wished it would never end.

A bothersome whistle rattled the kitchen windows.

"I'm afraid yer water kettle is boiling again, lass." Thomas pulled away, grinning.

Margaret rushed to the stove. "I guess I forgot to turn off the burner." She touched her fingers to a warm cheek, all but ashamed of what she felt inside. She smoothed out her skirt and got back to the task at hand. "Ok, you can make the cornbread cakes, and I'll fetch the chow-chow from the pantry."

"What on earth is chow-chow?"

"You've never had chow-chow? It's relish for the peas. You'll love it."

"Somehow, I don't doubt that. I seem to be falling in love with almost everything in this kitchen."

Margaret put a palm to her hot cheek. Surprise turned to relief and she smiled. She disappeared into the pantry.

~*~

"Margaret, Thomas, that was a mighty fine meal." Papa scooted his chair back and rested his hands on his belly.

"Thank you, Papa."

"Aye, thank ye, but yer daughter did most of the work. I did make a fine mess of yer kitchen though."

Mama, June, and Papa laughed.

But as of late, Elizabeth sulked and pushed black-eyed peas around on her plate instead of joining in the fun.

Margaret couldn't remember the last time she'd heard her sister's laugh. She sighed and put her hand over Thomas's. "That's not true. You cooked the cornbread all by yourself."

"It was good too." June patted her tummy.

"Why, thank ye, June."

Margaret stood and clapped her hands together. "OK, everyone, it's time to begin our second week of Advent."

Jeremiah clapped his hands.

June jumped up from her chair. "Come on, everybody. It's time to light the candles!"

Margaret hung behind with Mama, waiting for Elizabeth, who remained in her seat, staring at the plate of food. She hadn't taken a bite. Mama put her hands on Elizabeth's shoulders. "Come on, Elizabeth, let's go celebrate Advent. It will be fun."

Elizabeth scooted her chair back before Mama could get out of the way.

"Careful now, Elizabeth, you almost knocked Mama over," Papa said from the doorway.

Without acknowledging Papa, Elizabeth joined the rest of the family. She sat outside the circle everyone had made around the Advent wreath and candles.

Margaret took a seat next to Thomas and reached for the Bible that was already set out. "OK, Thomas, remind everyone what this week is supposed to be about."

He took her hand and squeezed it. "The second week of Advent is to remember Bethlehem and the love of God in sending His Son to save us."

Margaret opened the Bible. "This week, we'll be

reading from the book of Luke, chapter two, verses eight through fourteen." She began reading. *"And there were in the same country shepherds abiding in the field, keeping watch over their flock by night. And, lo, the angel of the Lord came upon them, and the glory of the Lord shone round about them: and they were sore afraid. And the angel said unto them, Fear not: for, behold, I bring you good tidings of great joy, which shall be to all people. For unto you is born this day in the city of David a Savior, which is Christ the Lord. And this shall be a sign unto you; Ye shall find the babe wrapped in swaddling clothes, lying in a manger. And suddenly there was with the angel a multitude of the heavenly host praising God, and saying, Glory to God in the highest, and on earth peace, good will toward men."* She closed the Bible. "Thomas, will you say the prayer for us this evening?"

"Of course I will." He blessed their family and the holiday with a heartfelt prayer.

Papa lit a small stick and returned to the table. He took Jeremiah's hand and placed the burning stick in it. Jeremiah's eyes were wide in silent awe as he lit the first and second candles.

The whole family joined in, deciding what song to sing with this scripture.

Elizabeth rose and went out the front door.

Mama turned to Papa, her lip quivering. "What are we gonna do, Jeb?"

Papa stood and blew out the candles.

Jeremiah looked as though he would cry, but instead poked out his bottom lip and pouted.

"Let's put this away for tonight. I'll go after Elizabeth and try to figure out what's going on inside that head of hers." Papa seemed grim.

"Thank you, Jeb." Mama said the words through

sniffles and tears. "June, will you help me put these candles and such away?"

"Yes, ma'am."

"Don't worry about the kitchen, Mama. Thomas and I will do the cleaning. Won't we, Thomas?" Margaret smiled at her beau.

"Of course, ma'am, we'll take care of it. Don't ye worry about a thing."

"But, but you two already cooked the meal. You shouldn't have to do the cleaning too." Tears trickled down Mama's cheeks.

"It'll be all right, Mama. We'll get through this. Remember that scripture you always quoted to me when I was going through my bad times?" Mama nodded and Margaret smiled. "Say it with me."

"Greater is He that is in you, than he that is in the world."

Mama put her hand on Margaret's. "I know those words are true, but everything seems so hopeless with Elizabeth."

"I know, Mama. I'll talk to her and see if I can smooth things over. It's me she has bad feelings for, so I'm the one who should talk to her."

"I want you to be careful what you say around her, Margaret. I'm afraid for her. She don't seem...right, you know, in her mind."

Fear and sadness welled up inside Margaret. Something she'd been thinking about for weeks sailed to the front of her mind and wouldn't go away. *Everyone is in agreement. Something is seriously wrong with Elizabeth.*

19

"Elizabeth, I'm coming in." Margaret called before she opened the door. Elizabeth sat at the old oak desk between their two beds. She had a pencil in her hand and was writing in her journal.

Margaret eased over to her bed and fluffed the pillows before sitting on the edge, facing her sister.

Elizabeth stopped writing and turned toward her. Margaret couldn't believe what she was seeing...Elizabeth was smiling at her.

She instantly felt relief at the warm reception. "What are you writing?" Margaret asked, hoping in her heart that this was the beginning of a turning point for her sister.

"It's a poem I wrote about the war. I wrote it for Mr. Langley. I thought it might make him feel better. He gets very sad, you know."

Margaret couldn't help but notice how Elizabeth's voice didn't even sound like her own. There was simply too much happiness for this to be her sister talking.

"That's very sweet of you, Elizabeth." Margaret put her fists on the bed, bracing herself. "I'm also very proud of how you've been going to help Mr. Langley with his son. I'm sure it's not easy caring for him without anyone to help him. He's very lucky to have you."

Elizabeth didn't acknowledge what she'd said. "Would you like to read my poem? I think it's really good." Elizabeth talked over Margaret.

"I'm sure it is, and I'd love to read it, but first I'd like to talk to you."

Elizabeth shrugged her shoulders and went back to writing.

Margaret took a deep breath as she approached the touchy subject. "Elizabeth...even though I'm proud of how you've helped Mr. Langley, I'm also worried about the way you've been acting lately."

"I don't know what you're talking about." She didn't look at Margaret when she answered and continued writing. "I don't think I've been acting any differently than I always have. I'm fine...actually, I feel better than ever."

At this moment Elizabeth did seem fine.

"Yes, you do seem fine...now, but lately you've been so sharp with everyone, even Mama and Papa, and you run off to the Langleys' without telling anyone where you're going. It's just not proper behavior for a young woman. When you went missing during the raid, I thought, well, to tell the truth, I thought it would be the end of Mama."

"Well, you can believe me when I say I was perfectly safe with Mr. Langley. But I know. I haven't been treating Mama and Papa with the respect they deserve."

Margaret was finally getting through to her, so she continued on. "And it makes me sad that you seem so upset about my relationship with Thomas. Why can't you be happy for us...especially after all I've been through since Jeffrey was killed?"

Elizabeth stopped writing and instead drew

images on the side of her paper. "Ever since we first came here, I've prayed every day for a boy to come into my life. Someone I could love and who would love me in return. When Mama and Papa brought Thomas here, I knew my prayers had been answered." She took her eyes off her paper and cast a dark look toward Margaret. "You see, God already gave you a chance at love and you lost it. It should have been my turn."

Elizabeth's words pierced through Margaret's heart. But she set her feelings aside to bring solace to her sister. It had been, after all, the first time anyone had gotten her to talk about anything in months.

"Elizabeth." Margaret smiled and tried to make light of the situation. "You're far too young to be thinking about men and marriage." She drew in a deep breath when she thought of a brilliant idea. "Oh, I know what we can do. Just wait until we return to New Orleans. We'll get ourselves a couple fine gowns and go to a ball. Now doesn't that sound like a marvelous idea? You'll be able to meet young men...but of course, you'll have to wait until you're of the right age."

Margaret's words didn't provide the results she'd hoped for. Elizabeth's lighthearted expression when she came into the room was turning into what looked like pure misery. Her shoulders fell with her countenance. She pressed so hard with her pencil that it carved a hole through the pages of her journal.

Margaret didn't know what to do. On one hand, her heart ached for her sister, but on the other hand, she almost felt afraid of her. What had she done to cause such a reaction from her?

Elizabeth glared. Desperation sounded in her voice. "Don't you realize we're never going back to

New Orleans? Thanks to this stupid war, we're never going to know any happiness ever again. We're stuck here on this godforsaken peninsula for good."

"Don't talk like that, Elizabeth. I know we'll return to New Orleans. But in the meantime, I'm trying to make things better for all of us while we're here. I have some fun things planned for the rest of Advent. I want everything to be perfect for Thomas's last few weeks with us. You know he'll be leaving shortly after Christmas."

"That's just fine with me. The sooner he leaves the better. Everything has been terrible since he's been here—especially you."

"What do you mean by that?"

Elizabeth still didn't make eye contact with her. "You know exactly what I mean. The way you showed yourself off to Thomas when he first came here is nothing but shameless. And don't think I don't know what you let Thomas do to you when y'all are alone together. You both should be ashamed."

Margaret shot up from the bed. Her blood boiled from within. "I have done no such thing. And how dare you talk about Thomas that way. He has never been anything but a perfect gentleman toward me. Now you need to apologize…right this instant."

"The only one that's going to apologize is you…when God punishes you. And if He doesn't do it soon, then maybe I will do it for Him."

Margaret was speechless. She watched her younger sister get up and leave the room, slamming the door behind her. It felt as if a stranger had just walked past. Margaret didn't even know her own sister anymore. She went to the desk and peered at the undecipherable marks her sister had scrawled. She noticed the single piece of paper upon which Elizabeth had written her poem. Margaret picked up the poem.

North versus South, state against state,
The South wanted freedom, the North gave them hate.
Cries of indignation, a southern son dies in vain,
Death on both sides, blood flows as rain.

Margaret stopped reading and sank onto the chair, clutching her stomach. Bile rose in her throat. She took the poem, folded it, and tucked it into her apron. Elizabeth could not show this to Mr. Langley. *If I'd lost my son…actually he's lost both his sons to the war…Oh, my goodness. This might just send the poor man on to the Promised Land.* She swiped away tears that threatened. There was no time for crying now. She had to figure out what to do with the poem and with Elizabeth. Should she tell Papa…Mama…Thomas? But her time with Thomas was drawing to an end and she didn't want to ruin what little time they had left. She had about as much control over Elizabeth as she did over the mighty Gulf of Mexico. The thought that Elizabeth could end up like Cousin Emma scared her more than anything.

20

Margaret stood next to Papa at the kitchen table. They waited for Mama to finish checking on the two youngest children playing in the front room. Since there was no bossiness heard from June and there was no crying heard from Jeremiah, Margaret assumed they were playing nicely together.

Mama joined them in the kitchen. "OK, Jeb, you've got Thomas busy outside, right?"

"Yep. He shouldn't come up for at least an hour or two."

"Papa, you don't have to be so hard on him." Margaret was disturbed that Thomas might be doing too much. He was mostly healed, but he still had twinges of pain when he worked too hard.

"Child, he's fine. All right, tell us how to make this special Irish dish," Mama said.

"OK, I've set out everything we need to make the colcannon. We have to use collard greens, even though the recipe calls for kale or cabbage. But since we don't have either, the greens will have to do."

"I'll fetch a pot to boil the collards in." Mama retrieved the big pot from beneath the cabinet.

"Thank you, Mama."

"Well, what do you want me to do, Margaret?"

She smiled at her papa. "I really just wanted you to find something to keep Thomas busy while we cook up his favorite meal."

"Whew! Thank goodness, I thought I would have to help cook." Papa poured a cup of coffee before taking a seat at the table.

The water began to steam and Margaret added the collards, onions, and cubed potatoes to the pot. Mama added a few pinches of salt. "I don't know what's so special about boiled collard greens and potatoes, but if it's what the Irish folk like…"

"It's more than likely that cabbage and potatoes is all they had available to them. And if that's all you have, then you might as well develop a likin' for it." Papa sipped his coffee.

Mama pulled out the big slotted spoon and handed it to Margaret. "You're probably right about that, Jeb. Thomas's people went through some hard times, for sure."

Margaret stirred the steaming concoction. "I would have liked to make it just like his mama did, but we don't have the right kind of greens. Oh well, this will have to do."

Mama patted her on the shoulder. "I'm sure he'll like it just fine."

"Sure would be nice if we had enough coffee to make a strong pot again." Mama poured a cup of coffee for herself and looked at Papa. "Jeb, have you seen any of that wild chicory growing on the property lately?"

"No, but I can take a look around if you'd like."

"It would sure make this coffee taste better." She sighed. "If we ever go back to New Orleans, I want you to take me to that new coffee shop that was opening in the French Market. What was the name of it?"

"Café Du Monde," Margaret answered.

"Yes, that was it." Mama nodded.

June and Jeremiah laughed and carried on in the front room.

Mama rested her chin on her palm. "Wonder where Elizabeth has run off to this time."

"She's down at the Langley place," Margaret said.

Papa pushed back from the table. "You know, it just ain't right for a young girl to be going over to a man's home...alone."

"Oh, Jeb, he's harmless." Mama took another sip.

"That's not the point. It just don't look right." He set his cup down. "I should put a stop to it."

Margaret turned to the cook pot.

"I've tried to get her to stop going over there, but every time I do, she flies into a rage. She says Mr. Langley is the only person who really understands her." Mama was pensive.

"That's just crazy talk!" Margaret dropped the spoon into the pot. "Oh, Mama, I didn't mean to say that Elizabeth is crazy. It's just...how can Mr. Langley be the only one who understands her?"

"She really is starting to act like your cousin Emma."

Papa nodded but didn't make eye contact with Mama. He just sat there, circling the rim of his cup with his index finger.

"It's OK, Margaret. Papa told me the same thing he told you. We need to face the fact that Elizabeth has a problem."

Margaret pulled out a folded piece of paper. "I...I wasn't sure whether or not I should show this to you."

"What is it, Margaret?" Papa held out his hand. He opened the paper, and together her parents read the disturbing poem Elizabeth had written. Papa folded the paper and handed it back to Margaret.

"Papa…she told me she wrote it for Mr. Langley."

Mama's brow rose. "Don't you dare give that back to her, Margaret. For heaven's sake, we can't let him read that."

Dread crept into Margaret's heart. "Mama, Papa, what will we do if Elizabeth gets any worse?"

"I don't know, darlin'. We haven't thought that far ahead yet." Papa tapped his finger on the edge of his coffee cup, a nervous gesture Margaret had never noticed before.

"If only we had a doctor here on the peninsula we could take her to. But there's not even a minister we could talk to." Mama looked on the verge of tears.

Papa reached up and took her hand. "It's going to be all right, Caroline. We'll get through this…somehow, we are going to get through this."

Margaret wished that what Papa said was true, that they were going to get through this. Would Elizabeth's condition continue to get worse? And if it did, would they have to lock her away inside her room? *I wonder what ever happened to Emma?*

~*~

"All right, Mama, it's time for you to give me your ring." Margaret was so excited she wanted to jump up and down. "I already have the thimble, the button, and the coin. I just need your ring and the colcannon will be ready to eat."

"I'm surprised at how good it smells." Mama twisted and turned the ring on her finger. "My finger must be swollen. I'm having a hard time getting it off." The stubborn ring finally popped over her knuckle and landed on the floor.

Margaret picked it up. She leaned over the bowl of creamed potatoes, onion, and collard greens, ready to drop the four items into the food.

"Now, if you lose my wedding ring, I might have to tan your hide, little lady," Mama teased.

"We're not going to lose your ring."

"Well, you better not," she answered with a smile. "Now move over and let me dish out a bowlful for Jeremiah before you put all those trinkets in."

"Oh, right, you don't want him getting hold of these things!"

Margaret closed both hands around the cache, lifted them to her chin, and shut her eyes. *O Lord, I know this game is all for fun and we don't believe in chance. But, Lord, if it be Thy will, may I please be the one to get the ring? In Jesus's name, amen.*

21

Thomas spent the entire afternoon mending pens, pulling weeds, and sweeping everything from the front porch to the shed. He was thankful for the work Mr. Logan gave him. It felt good to earn his keep, but it made him a bit curious as to why he had been told to stay out of the house. Something was afoot. Nevertheless, a good day's work made for an honest man.

"Thomas, Elizabeth, supper's ready," Mr. Logan called.

The sound was music to his ears as he'd worked up a powerful appetite. When all the tools were put away, he headed inside. The house had a scent of something familiar. It smelled like...home. Thomas's spirits lifted...was this becoming home? "I didn't see Elizabeth outside, sir. Don't think she's around."

Mr. Logan patted his shoulder. "All right, Thomas, go on in and have a seat."

Mrs. Logan bounced Jeremiah on her hip. June stood on tiptoe behind a chair. The roughhewn table was set to perfection with their best dishes. And the finest thing in the room was Margaret, but right now, Thomas didn't know what looked better, the gorgeous young woman or the great bowl of food she held in her arms.

"Is that what I think it is, Margaret dear?"

"It sure is."

"Colcannon…and it's not even Hallowe—"

"Elizabeth, it's suppertime," Mr. Logan hollered out the kitchen door.

After washing his hands, Thomas settled into his seat.

The rest of the family had taken their regular places. Silence filled the room.

Thomas looked at Margaret. "I can't believe ye did this for me. Did ye even add the charms I told ye about?"

"We sure did…even Mama's ring." Margaret's expression changed.

"What is it, lass?"

"I'm sorry to tell you that it won't be quite the same because we don't have kale or cabbage, so we had to use collard greens."

He laughed. "Well then, this will be your own special recipe. I suppose it will be forever known as 'southern colcannon.'"

Mr. and Mrs. Logan laughed.

"Don't ye worry a bit. I'm sure it will be the best I've ever tasted."

"Papa, it doesn't look like Elizabeth is coming. May we please start without her?" Margaret asked.

"I reckon we ought to." Mr. Logan asked Thomas to say the blessing.

Thomas said a prayer of thanksgiving for the family who cared so much for him they would make a dinner especially for him. He also took special care to pray for Elizabeth's safe return.

June dug into her bowl with fervor. Thomas remembered what fun it had been for him and his brothers to find the tokens as children. The memory was warm and he treasured it in his heart.

"What in tarnation is this?" Mr. Logan pulled the potato-covered thimble out of his mouth. "I 'bout near chipped a tooth on that thing." Mr. Logan overacted and they all broke out in laughter.

"Jebediah, stop your silliness." Mrs. Logan hid her grin.

"Tell us what the thimble means, Thomas," June begged.

He dragged a towel across his mouth and smiled, half because the little redhead had asked so sweetly and half because it was the first time she ever called him by his first name. "Well, I'm so sorry to tell ye, Mr. Logan, but the thimble means yer going to be an old maid." Thomas started laughing.

June laughed hysterically.

Margaret covered her own smile, while Mrs. Logan rolled her eyes and shook her head.

When it seemed the revelry couldn't get any livelier, Mr. Logan pulled the bright, shiny coin from his mouth.

He looked at his youngest daughter; her eyes grew wide with excitement. "Can't a man get a decent meal around here anymore?"

Again, June burst with laughter, her red curls bouncing up and down. Jeremiah laughed too, even though he was too young to know what they were all laughing about.

"Looks like a right 'rich' meal if ye ask me." Thomas smiled at his own pun.

"Papa, you're a rich old maid!" June pointed at her father and chortled.

"Hush up, June," Margaret scolded, still grinning.

It warmed Thomas's heart that the family could

share in one of the fonder customs of his childhood. The empty place across from him was an ever-present reminder of the growing tension between Elizabeth and her family. He couldn't quite figure out what affliction was taking place in the poor child's mind, but whatever was happening to her was a burden on the entire family. He was glad one of his own traditions could brighten their day, even if it was fleeting.

After the laughter quieted, the conversation drifted to the family's goat, Nanny Sue.

"I've noticed that yer nanny goat is beginning to lose her milk, sir. What's the possibility of getting her bred soon?"

Mr. Logan stirred the remains of his bowl. "I've come to notice that myself. I need to take a walk down to the Goodman place to see whether or not he lost his ram in the raid." He scooped up a bite. "I sure hope not. I'll make my way down there before week's end."

"Aye, that'll be good."

Mr. Logan made a strange face. He spoke with his mouth full of potatoes. "You're not going to believe this." Then he pulled the button out of his mouth. "Caroline, you didn't give me anything but a bowl full of trinkets!"

"Oh, hush up, Jebediah!" She grinned at her husband. "You better not have my wedding ring hidden in that bowl too."

"I'd rather have another bowl without so much extra stuff in it, if you don't mind." Mr. Logan held his bowl out to his wife.

"Papa, you got everything." June huffed. "I didn't get one blessed thing in my bowl of cannon." She crossed her arms. "How in the world am I gonna have any money or get married or anything?"

"Aw, come on now, June." Thomas hugged the little girl. "It just goes to show ye, there's no such thing as good luck...only the blessings of God. Besides, there's still one more charm left to be found and ye haven't finished yer bowl yet."

Thomas's words were enough to prompt her to dig into the hearty meal. She turned to her papa and taunted him. "Ha, ha, ha, I'm gonna find the last charm before you do!"

"Watch it, young lady," Mr. Logan warned as he began to eat again, checking each bite carefully.

So much attention had been given to Mr. Logan and June that Thomas had neglected the most important person at the table...Margaret. Thomas turned to ask her how she liked her first meal of colcannon.

Before he could get the words out, he noticed her hand reaching up to her mouth.

Every noise in the kitchen seemed to fade away from Thomas's hearing as he waited with bated breath for his lovely Margaret to announce her discovery.

Raven tresses fell onto the bodice of her emerald dress. She gently removed her mother's wedding band from between her lips. She gazed at it, and then hugged it to her heart. She then looked heavenward, closing her eyes she mouthed the words...*thank You*.

22

Margaret's heart was still aflutter after finding the wedding ring in her bowl. She put away the clean dinner dishes in silence, dreaming of her future.

"What's wrong with you, Margaret?" June put her hand on her hip. "I just dried that bowl and you put it back in the dishwater."

Margaret chuckled at her mishap. She leaned over to her sister's ear and whispered, "Can you keep a secret?"

"Uh-huh." June's eyes grew with excitement.

"I got the wedding ring in my bowl of colcannon. That means someone is going to ask me to marry them."

June turned Margaret's head so she could whisper into her ear. "I bet it's gonna be Thomas."

"Oh, I hope you're right." She straightened and handed the bowl back to June for drying.

All the dishes were clean, except for Elizabeth's. Mama had scraped what remained of the colcannon into her bowl and left it on the table, waiting for her to return.

Margaret thought about her sister, wondering once again what they were to do as a family for her. *Elizabeth, what is happening to you? Why are you acting this way? Are you ever going to get better?*

Her sadness over Elizabeth's plight led her heart down a melancholy path—and so close to Christmastime. Thomas's departure was drawing ever closer with each passing day.

"Come on, June, it's time for the Advent candles." She took June's hand and went into the other room, determined to make the best of these last few days with Thomas.

The glow of lamplight warmed the area where Mama, Thomas, and Jeremiah gathered, ready to start the service.

Papa opened the front door. "Elizabeth," he hollered.

"Jeb, she won't be able to hear you if she's at Langley's place," Mama murmured.

Papa stepped away from the door and took his coat off the hook. "That's it. I'm going over there." His eyes revealed worry.

"She's coming up the road!" June had gone out to the porch, but ran back in with the news.

Tension eased out of Papa's shoulders.

Margaret handed Thomas the Bible.

He started flipping through the pages.

June plopped down next to them.

Elizabeth came through the door as if she were sneaking in late for church service. A sudden gust of bitter-cold air followed her into the room. The mood of everyone seemed to change in an instant with her arrival.

Margaret clutched her arms against the cold.

Elizabeth's eyes met Papa's, and she froze.

Papa shut the door behind her. "We're going to have ourselves a long talk after this service. You understand me, young lady?"

"Yes, sir." Elizabeth kept her back arrow-straight as she walked across the room and took a seat next to Mama.

Papa turned his attention to Thomas and gave him a nod.

"All right, now the third week of Advent is to remember the shepherds who were the first to hear the joyous announcement of Christ's birth. Tonight I'll be reading from the book of Luke." Thomas smiled at his listeners. "'*And she brought forth her firstborn son, and wrapped him in swaddling clothes, and laid him in a manger; because there was no room for them in the inn. And there were in the same country shepherds abiding in the field, keeping watch over their flock by night. And, lo, the angel of the Lord came upon them, and the glory of the Lord shone round about them: and they were sore afraid.*'" Thomas's tone deepened.

"Ha, ha, ha, ha, ha! Afraid. That's so funny!"

Thomas stopped reading and turned to Elizabeth. Everyone else in the room looked at her as well.

Mama leaned forward and put her hand on her daughter's knee. The obvious smile she tried to paste on her face wasn't doing its job. Her lips quivered. "Elizabeth…what's so funny, dear?"

Elizabeth's eyes were as wild as a cornered animal. "Thomas made me think about how afraid everybody will be in the morning when the soldiers arrive."

For a moment, the entire family was frozen.

Margaret stood.

Thomas reached out and put his arm around her waist to draw her close. June raised her arms to him and he brought her into his lap.

Papa stepped inside the circle of light put off by the oil lamp. His countenance was grave. "Look at me,

Elizabeth. Do you know something about another raid?"

"Not *those* kind of soldiers, Papa!" Elizabeth looked at Papa, then put her hand to her mouth and started to giggle for no apparent reason.

"Oh dear…Elizabeth, what have you done?" Mama swung Jeremiah to the floor and stood.

"How long did you expect me to hide this little plot of yours, Mama? I waited as long as I could, but I had to tell someone. Mr. Langley was all but speechless…the very idea that we would hide a Yankee sailor right here in our home with a fort full of Confederate soldiers right down the road. He couldn't believe his ears."

"Oh, Jeb…" Mama's voice was weak.

Papa walked over to the side table and picked up his pipe, tobacco pouch, and matches. The front screen door opened and slammed shut. The sound of one of the rocking chairs creaked on the porch and then a match was struck. Through the window, the lantern's light glowed.

"And…Mr. Langley said he's going over to Fort Greene at the first sign of light in the morning to inform them of your…what did he call it? Oh yes— treason." Elizabeth was calm.

"Do you have any idea what you've done?" Margaret shouted. "Don't you realize that if one of us is arrested for treason, we'll all go to jail? Not only that, Thomas will be sh-shot, or hanged." A stream of tears flowed down her cheeks at the sudden realization. "Elizabeth! I can't believe you would do such a thing. Papa is right…you are crazy!"

Mama gasped. "Margaret, don't talk like that." She then turned to Elizabeth. "She didn't mean what she said. Papa would never say such a thing." Mama's hand flew to her mouth, and she started to choke on a flood of tears.

"Mama, I don't need you to explain my actions to Elizabeth. She is completely to blame here. And I sure don't see anyone trying to explain what caused her to do the unthinkable."

Mama collapsed onto her chair. "Oh, Elizabeth, why have you done this to us?"

"Ma, Ma, Ma, Ma," Jeremiah mournfully whined, his head lying on Mama's lap.

No longer able to look at her sister, Margaret turned to Thomas.

He held his arm out to her while holding tight to little June. She rushed to his side and fell into his embrace.

"Why would Lizbeth do such a bad thing?" June ran to Mama.

"I don't know, honey. I just don't know." Mama caressed her hair.

Papa pushed through the front screen door, and it slammed behind him.

"Caroline, dry your face and pull yourself together. We've got a lot of work to do and very little time to do it. Elizabeth, I don't want to see you for the rest of the day." He pointed toward the room the three sisters shared. "Now get in there and don't come out."

Elizabeth went toward the bedroom door, then stopped. "It's too late, Papa. There's nothing you can do to change what's been done."

"Leave the room…now!"

She slammed the door behind her.

"June, take Jeremiah into our room and lay down on the bed with him. Hopefully, he'll take a nap." Papa shooed her and Jeremiah into their room.

"Thomas, I'll go talk to Mr. Langley. Maybe I can make some kind of deal with him, if he agrees not to go to the fort." Papa was determined.

"I don't understand. What kind of deal would you make with him?" Margaret asked.

"I don't know, Margaret. Maybe I could offer to do some work for him or give him something of value in exchange for his silence."

Margaret nodded.

Papa turned his attention back to Thomas. "Either way, I think you should prepare to leave, son."

Margaret began to shake, terrified that she would soon be bawling. "But I'm not ready for Thomas to leave. Not now—not yet. We were supposed to have our first Christmas together."

Papa ignored her. "Caroline, go pack up enough food to carry Thomas over for a few days."

Mama wiped her eyes and headed for the kitchen.

"Mr. Logan, I think it's best if I leave right away...tonight. That way, if the soldiers come, you can deny ever having me here. I don't want anything to bring harm to this family or the woman I love." He looked at Margaret and stroked her hair. "Let me go and gather up a few things."

Margaret's body swayed and her head began to pound. She put her arms out to steady herself, but there was nothing to hold on to. "Oh, Papa, I can't breathe!"

Papa put an arm around her waist. "Steady, girl." He guided her to a chair and took hold of her hands. "All right now, slow and easy, take a breath, in and out."

The room stopped spinning and she was able to

breathe again.

"There we go." Papa lifted her chin. He spoke to her from a faraway place. "Look at me, Margaret. This isn't the end. I know Thomas will find a way to come back for you. He loves you. Now, if you love him, you will help me get him away from here as quick as we can. Listen to me. Thomas can...not...be...here if Old Man Langley goes and reports him to the soldiers at the fort. This is something we have to do to keep Thomas safe. I'm sorry, honey, but there's no other way."

Something clicked inside Margaret's mind. She sat up straight. "You're right, Papa. We need to get him out of here...now."

"Good girl, now come give me a hand getting things ready."

Margaret grabbed his arm. "Papa, promise me you won't let them find Thomas."

"I'll do my best, honey."

"You don't understand, Papa. I thought I would surely die when I lost Jeffrey, but somehow I managed to go on. But now...I love Thomas so much more than I've ever loved anyone else before." Tears streamed down her cheeks. "Papa, I don't know what I would do if anything happens to Thomas."

"We're not even going to think that way. We've been through some mighty tough things in the past, and every time, God has seen us through."

Margaret heard what Papa said, and she truly did trust God in everything. But she knew in her heart that if anything happened to her Thomas, she didn't trust what she might do to herself...or to Elizabeth. And that frightened her more than anything ever had.

23

Had it been any other time, the magnificent golden sunset slowly melting into Galveston Bay would have fully captivated Margaret's attention. But today its beauty mocked. It would be the last sunset she would share with the love of her life, perhaps forever, should he be captured by Confederate forces. No, she couldn't enjoy it, not with Thomas being forced to leave, no…run for his life.

They stood behind the house where they'd spent so much of their alone time together, Thomas's strong arms wrapped around her. There were few words between them even though a thousand questions burned in her mind. Would it be the last time she felt his embrace? What would happen to him after he left the peninsula? Would he come back for her?

"Look at me, lass. Ye don't have to worry about me. I'll be fine, I promise. I plan to make my way back up north and check on my pap and brothers. Then I'll meet up with my unit and serve out the rest of my time in the Navy. Look at the bright side—there'll be a pot of back pay waiting for me to collect. Then I'll come back for ye, and we'll live like kings."

Margaret wanted to smile, but her heart, it was broken. "How can you be so lighthearted at such a time as this?"

"Because I don't want this to be a sad goodbye. Can't we just think of it as a farewell for now?"

She couldn't help that her lips quivered. "Shut up and kiss me before I start crying again."

He pressed his lips against hers. Then he clasped her face and looked deep into eyes that brimmed with the promise of tears. "Will you give me your word you'll wait for me, lass?"

"I—I promise...I'll wait for you." She wiped her eyes. "But only if you'll promise to come back for me."

"I promise with all my heart."

Someone approached.

Papa came out holding a lantern. He cleared his throat. "Well, son, I suppose we'd better go. I'm leaning on a hunch that Mr. Nagle's boat should leave for Galveston within the hour. If not, we might be up a creek." Papa scratched his head. "Soon as I get back, I'll head straight over to Langley's place. I'll tell him you're already miles away and there's no need to bother the men at the fort. Lord knows, they have enough to worry about defending our coast."

"Aye, sir, I'll be right along."

Margaret felt as if the air was sucked from her lungs.

Thomas put his hand against the back of her head and they shared another meaningful yet heart-wrenching kiss. "Goodbye, lass. Know that I'll always love ye."

"I love you too, Thomas." She barely got the words out.

Their figures faded into the darkness. Finally, the light from Papa's lantern disappeared from sight. And Thomas was gone.

~*~

Margaret came into the front room.

Mama opened her arms to let Margaret collapse into them.

They held each other, shaking and sobbing.

"Oh, Margaret, I can't help but feel I pushed you into Thomas's arms only to have your heart broken again."

"It's not your fault, Mama. I just don't know what I've done to deserve having my heart crushed again. Why is God punishing me like this?"

"Oh, honey, God isn't punishing you." She stroked Margaret's hair.

"I already lost a fiancé. That should be enough for one lifetime."

"Well, it's not for us to question what God does. And whatever happens, you must have faith that God is in control, and He knows what's best for us. You have to believe that, Margaret. Besides, I know Thomas will come back for you. He loves you too much not to."

"How can you know for sure, Mama?"

"I just feel it in my heart. God will bring Thomas back to you."

"I hope you're right, Mama." She wiped her eyes. "I just don't understand why Elizabeth hates me so much that she would do such a terrible thing to me, Thomas, and the family."

"I—I really don't think Elizabeth knows what she's doing, honey. I'm afraid you were right. Her mind is slipping away from us." Mama sniffed back tears.

Margaret reached up and wiped her cheek. "What are we going to do with her, Mama?"

"I don't know, honey…I just don't know."

"What if she gets worse? What if she tries to hurt June or Jeremiah? Will we have to lock her away like Papa's aunt would lock away his cousin Emma?"

"Don't even say that, Margaret. We just need to pray and hope she gets better, that's all."

"But what if she doesn't, then what?" Desperation tinged Margaret's words. "Why did they lock Emma away when she had her spells? How could that even help?"

"All my daddy's medical training didn't teach me a thing about how to handle insanity. No amount of stitches and splints can help mend the human mind. People locked their loved ones in a closet because it was all anyone knew to do. Emma's family did it so she wouldn't hurt herself…or the people who loved her." Mama covered her eyes as she continued talking. "I won't do it, Margaret. I won't lock Elizabeth away in a closet. There's got to be a better way."

"But what, Mama?" Margaret pushed Mama's hand away. "Answer me, Mama. What are we gonna do?"

"We'll cross that bridge when we come to it."

Margaret collapsed onto an overstuffed chair. A thought crossed her mind. "Mama, what ever happened to Papa's cousin, Emma? Does she still live with her parents in Louisiana?"

All the blood drained from Mama's face. She stared at a picture on the wall. "Margaret, I've never told anyone this, and it's not to be shared. Do you understand?"

"Yes, ma'am." Nerves fluttered.

"Emma's full name was Emma Margaret Caldwell. We named you after her."

"Why haven't you ever told me that before?"

"Folks don't talk about such things. We named you in memory of Emma. She's dead, honey...she hung herself."

Part Two

24

Thomas would walk until his feet bled, and then he would beg a ride on wagons heading north. It seemed he would never make it to New York. Finally, he arrived in Tennessee where he was told there were northbound train tracks.

He jumped a train along with a group of unsavory-looking characters. With his dirty, disheveled clothes and the scruffy growth on his chin, he wondered if those he rode with thought him one of their own. What would Margaret think were she to see him now?

For some strange reason it was comforting to think the lot of them were more than likely in the same boat he was. Jumping the train was illegal and ungodly, and it made him feel about as low as he ever had. But having no means to pay his way and needing to get back to his duty as a sailor, he asked God to forgive him, and he'd figure out a way to pay later.

After many long weeks of travel, Thomas arrived in Yonkers, New York, on a Sunday afternoon. Winter plunged its frigid hooks into the North. Dirty brown snow piled high on street corners and people walked about clad in layers of thick clothing.

The smell of soot and smoke from well-used chimneys saturated the air. Thomas rubbed his arms against the brutal cold. He longed to hold his beloved Margaret next to a warm fireplace but would have settled for a warm winter coat. The only thing that made this place desirable to him was that he didn't have to fear capture by the Rebels and that his family was nearby. The town seemed to go on as usual despite the war raging in the South.

The little row house where his father lived remained intact with its peeling paint and rotting eaves. The distinct smell emanating from the house confused Thomas, as he'd never known his pap to smoke meat before. His mouth watered with the wonderful smell of food. He rapped on the door. An elderly man answered, but it wasn't Pap. A streak of fear dashed through his heart.

"What'd you want?" The old man's eyes revealed his misgivings. His thick accent fell harsh on Thomas's ears.

It took Thomas a moment to collect his thoughts. "Ah, yes. I'm looking for my pa…my father. I used to live here with him. His name is Darby Murphy."

The look of suspicion melted from the man's face and he smiled. "Well, that must make you either Thomas or Jonathan then." He opened the door all the way and took Thomas's arm, ushering him inside. "Come in, come in. You're letting all the warm air out."

Thomas stepped inside the house. "The name's Thomas Murphy, sir. Jonathan's my brother."

The door was shut behind him. It was unclear how the man could possibly know his or his brother's name, but he was sure to find out soon enough.

The man looked Thomas up and down and rubbed his chin. "Thomas, eh? Well, you're mighty tall compared to your father. But you have that same Irish accent, that's for sure."

"Excuse me, sir. Ye sure seem to know a lot about me, but I haven't a clue who you are."

The man walked as if it pained him to get around.

Thomas followed him to the small kitchen table near the fire. He pulled out a chair and sat down.

"Well, of course, you don't; my apologies. The name's Gorski, Edward Gorski. But you can call me Ed." He moved to the stove and put a kettle on to boil.

Thomas looked around the familiar surroundings and found the source of the divine aroma.

"Son, don't you worry about your father. As best I know, he's fine."

A wave of relief flooded Thomas's heart despite the fact that his father so obviously wasn't living here. Where had he and Michael gone? He tapped impatient, cold fingers on the table. "So can ye tell me where my pap is, Mr. Gorski?"

Mr. Gorski waved off Thomas's question. "Just hold up there, young fellow. Let me make some coffee to warm your insides, and I'll tell you all about it."

The coffee did sound wonderful. There was probably no use rushing Mr. Gorski. He lifted his hands toward the fire, careful not to touch the slab of meat dangling from the hearth. The smell of the meat so close to his face was intoxicating.

After a few moments Mr. Gorski brought two mugs of coffee to the table. "Good ol' cup of coffee will warm you up. Oh, be careful of that pastrami—it's going on display in my shop window tomorrow." He set a mug in front of Thomas and placed the other on the table. He was about to sit in the chair, but jumped up. "Oh, my goodness, I almost forgot."

Gorski went to the countertop next to the stove. He dug through a stack of papers, looking for something. "Ah, here it is." He pulled out an envelope and brought it back to the table.

The envelope was plain and white with Thomas's name written on the front in ink. Thomas reached for it, recognizing his father's writing. "It's from my pap."

"Yes, sir, he left it with me before he moved on. But I'll let you read about that for yourself."

Thomas opened the flap, removed the letter, and began to read.

Dear Thomas, if you're reading this letter, then you went to the old house before going to the naval office. I left a letter for you with them as well so you would be sure and receive the message. I won't go into detail here, but Michael and I have moved up to Massachusetts. I pray that you will come to us as soon as you are able. Inquire for Michael at Massachusetts General Hospital in order to find us. Love, Pap.

"What on earth are they doing in Massachusetts? And why should I inquire at the hospital for them?"

His words were more for himself than Mr. Gorski, but the old man answered him anyway. "Well, I can't say that I actually knew your father. I took over his lease when he moved out. He left that letter with me and asked that I give it to you, should you show up." He took a sip from his mug. "Heavens, that's been almost eight months ago."

"Eight months…they've been gone for eight months?" He released a long, mournful sigh. He rested his elbows on the table and rubbed his eyes. "I've been on the road for so long, and now I have to keep going all the way up to Boston?"

Mr. Gorski walked to an icebox and removed a bowl of butter and a plate of sliced meat and set them in front of Thomas. He then gathered a knife, a plate, and a basket covered with a piece of cheesecloth and returned to sit at the table.

When he uncovered the basket, the wonderful aroma of fresh sourdough bread wafted to Thomas's nostrils.

Gorski took a slice and shoved the basket to him.

Thomas took a large piece and waited for his host to finish using the butter knife.

Gorski motioned toward the plate of meat. "Have yourself a big slab of that ham. My smoked meats are some of the best you've ever tasted. I guarantee it. Now, of course, I was able to get my hands on a lot more kinds of meat before the war, but that's how it goes, I suppose."

Thomas helped himself to some of the sweet-smelling ham. "Thank ye, sir. I'm much obliged." He laid the piece of meat on top of the bread he'd smeared with butter.

"Well, I can tell you haven't had much to eat by the way your clothes are hanging on your body. You're too big a man to be so skinny. Reminds me of my grandson; probably around your age."

The good food and warm coffee helped to soothe Thomas's beleaguered disposition. "Yer grandson, eh, does he live close by?"

"Not anymore," Mr. Gorski said quietly. "He was killed at Gettysburg back in sixty-three."

~*~

By the time evening rolled around, Thomas had heard the entire history of Mr. Gorski's family. After his daughter died in childbirth, he and his wife raised their grandson, and the three of them worked together in his butcher shop. He had to move into this place after a fire destroyed the apartment above his shop. Now with his grandson and wife gone, he was truly alone in the world.

Thomas stood up from the table and brushed sourdough crumbs from his trousers. "Mr. Gorski, I'm much obliged for yer kind hospitality, but I'm afraid I must be leaving now. I have a long way to go yet."

Mr. Gorski took a sip of coffee. "Thomas, why don't you sit back down. I have a proposition you might be interested in."

25

Thomas accepted Mr. Gorski's proposal of work in exchange for a bit of money and a place to rest up before continuing on to Boston. After only a short time training under Mr. Gorski, Thomas found himself proficient in the art of brining and smoking meats. It made for a good partnership. Thomas needed the money, the food, and a place to stay. And Mr. Gorski needed someone to talk to. And that's what he did from daylight until dark.

As the weeks passed, a hole grew in Thomas's heart. The absence of Margaret was unbearable. He needed her in his life...in his arms. Everywhere and everything reminded him of her. The purple robes portrayed on the stained glass in Mr. Gorski's parish were the color of her violet eyes. Coals cooling in the fireplace were as black as her raven hair. Even the fresh milk delivered to the butcher shop reminded him of Margaret's porcelain-colored skin.

It didn't help Thomas that New York was overflowing with war widows. The women who came in Gorski's shop were desperate to share their tales of loss with him. He listened out of sympathy.

Thomas was ready to leave. He waited for the right time to break the news to Mr. Gorski.

The two men chatted as dusk drew near. They ate

cheese and bread and drank strong coffee. They laughed and talked about family and friends.

Thomas backed his chair away from the table, full and satisfied. "Well, Ed, I can't thank ye enough for taking me in when I needed the rest. But I'm afraid the time has come for me to move on now."

Mr. Gorski rubbed his rough thumb on the handle of his coffee mug. "I was afraid you would say that. Can't say I didn't know it was coming. I'm sure you're anxious to see your family though." He looked at Thomas eye to eye. "When are you thinking about heading up north?"

"Soon, I'm afraid. I'm anxious to get up to Boston and see my pap and brother. But honestly, sir, I'm more eager to head back to Texas and hold my Margaret in my arms."

The older man chuckled and lifted his coffee mug to him. "Can't say that I blame you, son."

On the day he left, Thomas had so many farewells to say to all the nice people he'd met in New York, it seemed he would never get away. He hugged his elderly savior and promised to come back again someday. With Mr. Gorski's gift of a huge package of smoked meat thrown over his shoulder, Thomas went on his way.

~*~

The sun was beginning to set by the time Thomas arrived at the address he was given at Massachusetts General Hospital.

It took a minute for Thomas's father to realize who was standing at his door. Tears formed in his eyes and he openly wept as he took Thomas in his arms.

Pap looked as if he'd aged twenty years since Thomas had last seen him. Obviously, the months of not knowing either of his two eldest sons' fates had taken a toll on him.

"Let me look at ye, son." The older Mr. Murphy held Thomas at arm's length.

"It's so good to see ye, Pap."

Pap pulled away, put his arm around Thomas's back, and led him inside the house. "I can't believe yer actually here. That means the old man saved the letter I wrote you and Jonathan."

Thomas smiled and nodded his head. "Yep, he sure did."

The pair moved to the table and sat down.

Thomas put his pack of meat and belongings down.

Pap held one of Thomas's hands in both his own across the table. "I truly didn't think I'd ever be seeing you again, Thomas." He picked up a stack of papers and handed it to Thomas.

Thomas's heart sank when he read the endless list of soldiers still unaccounted for—his name and his older brother Jonathan's name were among the missing.

They mourned their loss together. Thomas prayed with Pap, pleading beyond any hope that there was a chance his brother had somehow survived. But he knew in his heart that it was a pure miracle that he had managed to stay alive.

"Pap, I'd prefer not to tell ye, but I was shot off a boat as well. All the way down off the coast of Texas."

"Is that so?" Pap ran his hand through a thinning shock of red hair. "Is Texas really as big as they say it is?"

"Believe me...I had to make my way across most of it, and let me tell ye, it's big, all right." He took a coffee mug from the kitchen counter. The smell of coffee drew him to the warm pot sitting on the stove. "Pap, I need to talk to ye about a couple things."

"Pour me a cup while yer up, son."

Thomas poured his father a cup of coffee.

"So what's on yer mind, boy?"

"Well, ye already know I was shot and fell off the boat, but what ye don't know is that if it weren't for a family by the name of Logan, I wouldn't be here to tell ye about it."

"Is that right? If ye would tell me where they live, I'd be most willing to send them my thanks."

"Yes, of course, but there's more." He scratched his ear. "Pap, the Logans live on a little strip of land called the Bolivar Peninsula, way down on the coast of Texas. Mr. Logan is a trained lighthouse keeper, but the light was torn down at the beginning of the war. Mr. and Mrs. Logan have four children. The oldest of the bunch is named Margaret. And...and...I've fallen in love with her, Pap." There, he had said it.

Pap looked off into the distance and slowly nodded his head.

"I intend to earn some money and buy her a ring. I'm going to ask her to marry me, Pap."

Pap rubbed his jaw. "Well, if ye love her, I suppose that's what ye have to do then."

Thomas stood to hug his father.

The door swung open.

Michael looked at Thomas and his jaw dropped. He ran inside and put his arms around Thomas so tight he could barely breathe. "I can't believe my eyes. You're really here in the flesh. It's so good to see ye, brother."

When Michael released his firm grip, Thomas hugged him and patted him on the back. Thomas let go and took a long, thorough look at his younger brother. "For heaven's sake, when did this happen?"

"What is that, brother?"

"When did my little brother grow into a man?"

Michael chuckled. "Oh, go on now."

"And look at this hairy chin on ye." Thomas rubbed his younger brother's scraggly beard.

"All right, you two have a seat. Thomas just arrived and I have a whole passel of questions."

Through Thomas's stories, Pap and Michael learned much about the Logan family. They laughed with gusto at his telling of June and Jeremiah's antics. They were saddened to hear the not-so-happy tale of Elizabeth's betrayal. Thomas didn't know how else to explain it other than to say the poor girl had a problem with her mind. But the one they heard the most about was his beautiful Margaret and how he pined after her and longed to marry her.

Pap made fresh coffee and set out a dish of rolls.

Thomas cut up some of the fine meats Mr. Gorski sent with him. Sitting around the table with Pap and Michael warmed Thomas's heart. He didn't allow himself to dwell on the thought that the three of them were more than likely all that remained of the Murphy family. Thomas rubbed his fingers along the smooth grain of the bare wooden table while answering an abundance of questions from Pap and Michael. Then it was his turn to ask the questions. "So tell me, Michael, how is it that you and Pap came to live in Boston?"

"Go on, Michael, tell him." Pap looked proud as a peacock, gesturing to his youngest son.

"Oh, stop it now, Pap." He turned to Thomas. "Ye know I was working at DeCamp Hospital in New York." Michael looked away for a moment. When he turned back, the look on his face revealed his mind had visited a very dark place. "That was a mighty bloody place, to be sure. Anyway, I learned so much from the doctors I worked with there that one of them, Dr. William Mills, thought it would be to my benefit if I could train with the professional surgeons here at Massachusetts General. So he made the arrangements." He stopped a brief moment and laughed. "But to my surprise, I found that I had much to teach the surgeons here of what I'd learned working on the injured coming from the front lines."

"You always were the smart one of the bunch."

"So when are you and this woman of yours going to get married?"

Thomas smiled at how his brother referred to Margaret. "I promised her I'd come back as soon as I looked in on my family."

"Aw, ye don't have to rush off now, do ye?" Michael reached over and squeezed Thomas's shoulder.

"No, no, I don't plan to leave right away." Thomas reached for his coffee mug. Now that he knew his family's fate, he wanted to leave as soon as possible, but he knew he couldn't do that to his pap. "Maybe the two of you can show me around this big old town."

The three men talked deep into the night. The night turned to day and the days turned to weeks.

One day, Thomas's heart told him it was time to leave.

His father and brother hated to see him go, but they understood him wanting to return to Texas and the woman he loved and intended to marry. They made him promise he would return someday soon with his bride. With his back pay from the Navy in hand, he set out for Texas.

26

April 16, 1865, Bolivar Peninsula, Texas

It was by no means reminiscent of the Easter feasts Margaret remembered from the past before the war broke out. But considering all they'd been through, especially in the past seven months since Thomas came into her life, she was thankful to have the hearty fish stew. There were many who were much less fortunate than the Logan family, so she faithfully prayed for them when she lifted daily prayers for Thomas's safe return.

Christmas had passed without the levity the season usually brought. They continued lighting the Advent candles in remembrance of Jesus...and in honor of Thomas.

Oh, how Margaret missed the feel of his strong arms around her waist as he whispered the words *I love you* in her ear. New Year's had come and gone without the brush of a midnight kiss from the one she loved. Then came the long months of icy, cold wind and rain that gripped the peninsula.

The little ones had been cooped up in the house so long they bolted at the first sign of spring. April's mild weather summoned forth an overabundance of sweet-smelling wildflowers that beckoned the two youngest Logans from the confines of the house. They wasted no time in picking as many of the native beauties as they could. The house took on a whole different look with Mama's water glasses filled with colorful flowers in every room.

Margaret watched her little brother and sister through the kitchen window as they played in the yard. The kitchen door flew open and banged against the wall. June and Jeremiah bounded inside. "Margaret, Margaret, look what me and Jer'miah made for you."

"Whoa, slow down now."

June smiled and batted her eyes as she presented Margaret with a whimsical crown they had laced together out of Indian blanket flowers.

"Aw, it's so beautiful." She took the braided flower wreath from June's hands. "Say…would you two mind if I took the flowers in to Elizabeth with her dinner?"

"Well, we made it for you." She turned to her little brother. "What do you think, Jer'miah? Should we let Margaret give the flowers to Elizabeth?"

The little boy looked up at his sisters. His sun-kissed cheeks glowed when he smiled at them. He nodded up and down without saying a word.

"Oh, thank you both so much. These beautiful flowers are sure to make Elizabeth perk right up. Don't you think?"

"I sure hope so. Papa said that girl's as low as a snake's belly," June pronounced.

"All right now, you two, better get back outside before Mama finds some chores for you to do."

June's eyes doubled in size. She grabbed Jeremiah by the hand and pulled him out the kitchen door. "See ya later," she hollered before they disappeared from Margaret's sight.

Margaret wanted to cry, realizing that even the little ones knew Elizabeth was in a very bad way. She placed the flowers around the small bowl of fish stew she had set out on a tray, thinking the beautiful yellow and orange colors might be just the thing to bring a little cheer to Elizabeth's heart. She sat at the kitchen table waiting for the kettle to boil for tea. It was the perfect opportunity to talk to God.

"Father God, I thank You for giving Your Son to die for us and for His glorious resurrection. Lord, please forgive me for my bitterness toward You after Thomas left. I know You don't promise us happiness in this world and to think You blessed me with having the chance to have loved and to have been loved by two wonderful, godly men—I never deserved that, Father. It's taken me a while, but I realize now that You were always in control. And this whole thing with Thomas probably came about so that Elizabeth's sickness could be revealed to us. Father, please forgive me for not trusting You fully. I'm not bitter anymore, and I'm ready to cast all my cares on You, because You're the only One who knows what's best for me...and Thomas. But, Lord, if it be in Your will, please let him come back to me." The teakettle whistle began to blow. She quickly ended their talk. "In Jesus's name, amen." Margaret picked up the tray of food and took it to the bedroom.

Elizabeth was asleep. Of late she slept more hours than she was awake.

"Happy Easter Sunday, Elizabeth. Jesus is risen." Margaret smiled because she didn't want anything to cause Elizabeth to feel any more sadness. It wasn't easy being cheerful when her heart was heavy for both Elizabeth and Thomas.

The room they shared had once smelled of rose water and talcum powder, but now smelled of urine and body odor. No matter how many times Mama cleaned, the smell wouldn't go away. The mattress was ruined.

Margaret and June moved into the front bedroom where Thomas had stayed. It was the only thing they could do to get away from the foul smell and woeful sounds their sister made all hours of the night.

Elizabeth stirred but didn't get up.

Margaret set the tray on the bureau and went to her bedside. "Come on, Elizabeth, it's time to wake up and have some food. You need to keep up your strength."

Elizabeth rolled over onto her back. She'd been crying. The once-chubby girl had wasted away to nothing.

Margaret physically lifted her sister to a sitting position in the bed.

Elizabeth trembled.

Margaret took a shawl from the bottom bureau drawer and draped it around her shoulders. "There, that should keep you nice and warm. Now stay right there while I get your food." She placed the tray over Elizabeth's lap, but her sister made no move to feed herself. Instead, she stared at Margaret with her sorrowful eyes.

"Come on now, eat up," Margaret said.

"How can you be so kind to me when I did everything I could think of to ruin your life and your life with Thomas?" Elizabeth's voice cracked as she spoke through dry and chapped lips.

"I don't know. I probably couldn't have if it weren't for the love of Jesus. I was so angry and hurt, but I talked to God about it. And finally, those feelings went away. But it took a while." She scooped up some broth and held it to Elizabeth's mouth.

"You know, Elizabeth, I've been doing a lot of thinking lately. And when you think about the Negro people and how much forgiveness they will have to muster up if they ever gain their freedom from slavery, then me forgiving you, my own flesh and blood, doesn't seem like that big a deal really."

Elizabeth grabbed Margaret's arm and pulled her close. She seemed to be crying but no tears flowed. "Can you please find it in your heart to forgive me, Margaret? I know what I did was wrong. I'm sorry. But...but." The words left her.

Margaret stroked some hair away from Elizabeth's face. "I accept your apology, but I already forgave you a long time ago. I couldn't go on like that." She put her hand on Elizabeth's frail arm. "You're my sister, and I love you." She picked up the teacup and gave Elizabeth a drink. "Besides, I tried my best to stay mad at you, but I just couldn't do it." Margaret smiled at her, but Elizabeth didn't smile back.

"I need to tell you something, Margaret."

"Wh-what is it?"

"There's something wrong with me." Elizabeth shook her head. "I don't understand it, but when I close my eyes, I see the most horrible images in my mind. I feel so hopeless. It's like...it's like I've wandered into an old, dark, abandoned house, and I can't find my way out. And sometimes I don't even have the will to go on living anymore, and I think about ways to...to..." She fell silent.

Margaret felt her stomach tighten. "Oh, you don't mean that, Elizabeth. You have your whole life ahead of you. Things will get better, I promise. When the war is over, things will go back to the way they were. We can start over. Everything will be all right. You just wait and see."

Elizabeth lifted the tray of food from her lap. With hands that shook, she handed it back to Margaret. Warm soup and tea spilled everywhere, even on the bedclothes.

"Elizabeth, be careful."

Elizabeth rolled over, turned her back to Margaret, and pulled the quilt over her head.

Margaret rose from the bed with the tray. She left the room and shut the door with her foot. Leaning against the door, her body shook as she fought back tears. *Oh, Father God, it's Easter Sunday and Christians all over the world are celebrating Your Son's glorious resurrection.* Tears flowed down her cheeks and neck. *But not even the risen Savior can bring happiness to the heart of our poor Elizabeth.*

27

Margaret placed Elizabeth's food tray, toppled soup and all, on the kitchen counter and went outside.

Mama and Papa sat on the front porch in rocking chairs. They seemed to enjoy the beauty that April had ushered in to the peninsula. Papa puffed on his pipe and Mama braided colorful strips of old rags, sheets, and clothing together for the rug she was making.

June and Jeremiah were all smiles, chasing a pair of baby ducks around the yard.

Necie brought the little birds by earlier that morning. "They gonna make a fine roast-duck dinner someday. If you ever get them away from those chil'ren, that is!" She threw back her head and gave a hearty laugh. Necie had been coming by to check on Elizabeth since Elizabeth had stopped going over to the Langley place. Sometimes Necie sat with Elizabeth, not saying a word, just patting her back and singing in a soft voice.

Margaret had no idea where the ducks came from, but everyone was very thankful for the gift.

Mama had asked Necie not to mention Elizabeth's illness to anyone else on the peninsula.

Margaret had told Necie the truth on one of her now-frequent trips to visit her at the Stoltzes' place. The slave girl didn't care in the least that Elizabeth was having mental issues. She simply accepted it and spent time soothing her friend.

Margaret took a seat in the rocking chair next to Papa. The sweet aroma of his pipe tobacco swirled through the air.

June instructed Jeremiah how to sit on the ground with his legs spread wide apart. She sat opposite him, touching her feet to his, making a small containment area for the baby ducks. Their hysterical laughter was an indication that the duck feathers must tickle their legs.

"Look at those two filthy kids, Jeb." Mama tore a rag in two for the next section of the rug. "It all seems so long ago."

"What seems so long ago, Mama?" Margaret leaned forward in her chair to look at her.

"Oh, I was reminiscing with Papa about our Easter celebrations back in New Orleans. How we would all dress up in our finery for church." Mama's gaze wandered off to a place where memories lived. "And I can just taste all the wonderful food we had…the roasted ham hock and enough vegetables for an army. Goodness, we would just now be sitting down to our glorious meal."

"Well, those days are over, Mama." Margaret regretted her cynical tone as soon as the words were out of her mouth.

"I know, but I can dream, can't I? Besides, Papa's Bible reading was as good as any Easter service we've ever attended."

Papa coughed and blew out a long stream of smoke. "Well, I don't know about all that."

"Oh, Papa, you did a great job." Margaret patted his knee. A long sigh escaped. "I fixed a tray and took it in to Elizabeth."

"Thank you, dear. Did she eat anything?" Mama asked.

"Not much to speak of...but she talked to me this time."

Papa sat up. "Really now? What did she say?"

"She apologized...and begged for my forgiveness. I told her I already forgave her some time ago."

"Well, that's some progress at least." Mama wove the piece of torn cloth into the section she braided. "Now if she would just get up and join the family again..."

"Mama, Elizabeth isn't getting better. If anything, she's worse than before when she was causing so much trouble."

"How can you say that? She sure isn't bothering anybody now."

"Listen to me, Mama...Papa. Elizabeth said she doesn't have the will to live anymore. Does that sound like she's getting better?" Her voice began to quiver. "Do you hear what I'm saying? She feels so bad off that she wants to die." She swiped away a tear rolling down her cheek and turned her full attention to Papa. "I beg of you, Papa, we've got to do something for her. You don't want her ending up like Mr. Langley's son, do you?"

Mr. Langley's son had taken a turn for the worse after Elizabeth stopped coming to care for him. She truly had been helping.

Papa puffed on his pipe and looked off into thin air, perhaps thinking on how to answer her.

Mama kept on working on her rug.

"I believe it was last year some time I read an article in the *Houston Telegraph*. It could have been the year before, I don't remember, but there was an article about a hospital that opened up in Austin a few years back that can help treat people with problems like Elizabeth. I think it was called the Texas Lunatic Asylum," Papa said, his tone calm.

Hope rose in Margaret's heart. "Papa, if you think there's any way they can help, then we have to take Elizabeth there. Please, Papa."

"Our daughter is not a lunatic, Jeb. She just needs some rest and she'll be fine." Mama dropped the piece of cloth she was working into the rug. She scowled at Papa.

"Caroline, have you ever thought that if there had been a place like this for Cousin Emma, she might still be with us today?"

"What else did the article say, Papa?"

"Well, if I remember correctly, it said that the cure for this kind of illness is some kind of structured environment. I think they put the patients on some kind of daily routine where they have certain household chores and they can talk to doctors and other people who are in the same situation. I think it would be a good idea for Elizabeth so she can get her mind right again."

Mama dropped her handiwork on the porch and put her face in her hands, sobbing.

"What is it, Mama?"

"I know Elizabeth needs help…but." Mama's sobs took over.

"But what, Mama?"

"It's just that if we send Elizabeth away, then everyone will know she's crazy."

"What's more important, Mama, being embarrassed about your daughter or her getting the help she needs before she does something to hurt herself?"

Papa stood and walked to the edge of the porch. He tamped his pipe on the porch rail, sending a cloud of ashes floating into the wind. He turned toward them and leaned against the railing. "Caroline, you know Margaret's right. Elizabeth is sick and nothing we're doing is helping her one bit. She sits in that bed, day after day, refusing to eat or talk to us. Can't you see she's wasting away, honey?" He choked and turned his head. "If there's anything we can do so she doesn't end up like Emma, then I say we do it."

"So what do you think, Mama?" Margaret pleaded, hoping her mother would relent.

Mama sniffed back tears. "Whatever Papa decides…that's what we'll do."

"Then that settles it," Papa said. "I'll plan to take Elizabeth to Austin. With all the comings and goings over at the fort, I'd like to go before the end of the month. Caroline, start thinking about what she will need to be gone for a month or more."

"A month…or more?" Mama's face looked as if he'd said five years instead of one month. "But, Jeb, how will we ever pay for her to stay a whole month?"

"I don't know, but somehow God will provide. We've got to trust Him on this."

A heavy load seemed to lift from Margaret's heart. Elizabeth was finally getting the help she needed. Now Margaret's concern was Mama. She would have to help her mama to hold it together, at least long enough for Papa and Elizabeth to go on their way. Margaret could almost guarantee the next few weeks weren't going to be easy.

28

A nice breeze blew in the front-room windows, bringing with it the scent of spring.

Mama worked on sewing an extra dress for Elizabeth's trip to Austin.

Margaret mended a blanket for her.

The weeks following Easter flew by without incident.

Margaret spent most of her time spooning liquid into her sister's mouth so she wouldn't waste away. She also tried to keep Mama busy. The month of April was fading into history, and thankfully, the deep well of tears inside Mama seemed to have dried up. Margaret wondered if there would be more tears as the day of Elizabeth and Papa's departure drew near.

They prayed daily for God to end the war or at the least provide abundant crops for their survival.

The extra chores Margaret had taken on since Mama needed her more helped to keep her mind off Thomas. But the dreams usually came late in the night when she should have been sleeping. She floated on a cloud, wearing a long white dress. Thomas waited for her at an altar. He picked her up and carried her away in his strong arms. Oh, how she longed for his embrace. Then she would awaken, her cheeks burning as fire…her sheets wet with tears and sweat.

During the day she dared not dwell on the things she'd dreamed about. When she wasn't busy working, she sat with Papa, who kept a watchful eye on the activity at the fort and gave her daily updates on what he'd observed.

"Have you noticed there hasn't been a blockade runner pass through here in weeks?" He folded the newspaper he'd read more than once and dropped it on the floor.

"Haven't been able to get my hands on any new news lately either. Mr. Tillman at the dock seems to think something's going on. He said it's been a while since he's seen any activity—Union or Confederate."

The news only made Margaret worry even more about Thomas's safety. She'd given the situation over to the Lord so many times she'd lost count, and yet she still found no peace with it. Why couldn't she have the faith she needed to get through times like this? "Have you already forgotten about that ship that ran aground only a week ago, Papa?"

"Right. How could I forget...?"

The front screen door swung open. June flew in; her eyes were as wide as a scared rabbit. Her chest heaved up and down.

Mama looked up from her sewing. "Where's Jeremiah?"

June walked straight to Papa. "Me and Jer'miah was minding our own business, playing in the yard."

Papa took hold of her small hand. "All right, then why are you so out of breath?"

"And why is your dress torn?" Mama asked.

She took in a deep breath. "Well...like I said, me and Jer'miah was playing in the yard, collecting bugs. I borrowed a butter knife from the kitchen to dig in the dirt."

"June Marie, what have I told you about taking things from the kitchen to play with? Is Jeremiah all right? Is that how you cut your dress?"

"I'm sorry, Mama, but we didn't have nothing else to dig with. And don't worry about Jer'miah. He's fine. And no, I didn't tear my dress on the knife."

"Then how did you tear your dress?"

"I'm trying to get to that if you'll just let me talk!"

"Watch your tone, young lady," Papa warned.

"I'm sorry, Papa."

"You need to apologize to your mama."

She turned to Mama. "I'm sorry."

"Go on with your story," Mama said.

"OK, so me and Jer'miah was playing in the yard, collecting bugs." June started over and continued with her story. "I found this really big beetle. His back was colored green and orange and yellow, and he was so shiny. Well, Jer'miah was scared silly, but not me. I took that butter knife and scooped him right into my jelly jar."

"You took one of my preserve jars too?" Mama asked, her tone ominous.

June bowed her head and made a circle on the floor with her foot. "Yes, ma'am."

"Oh, for heaven's sake, June."

"Yep, Jer'miah's outside looking at that bug right now. Oh, and about my dress. When I was putting it on this morning, my foot got hung in the hem and that's how it tore."

"Young lady, you need to be more careful with your things. And you need to learn to keep your hands off my things."

"Yes, ma'am, I will." She leaned against Papa's

chair. "I thought y'all might want to know that there's a man coming up toward the house, and he ain't riding no donkey. He has an honest-to-goodness horse."

The three adults in the room sprang from their seats and headed for the door. Papa was the first outside, followed by Margaret and then Mama, who made a beeline for Jeremiah. She snatched him up off the ground and carried him onto the porch, the bug jar held tight in his hands.

Fear washed over Margaret at the sight of the man's Federal uniform, but if he was a one-man raiding party, he didn't look as if he could do much damage.

They had no time to hide even if they wanted to.

He didn't seem like a threat at all. His uniform was bright and clean and his horse was immaculately groomed. The horse trotted toward them. When he was less than a stone's throw away, the man dismounted his horse. The beautiful brown stallion nickered and shook his head. The man patted his muzzle, took the reins, and led him toward the house.

Papa stood straight while the young man approached.

June draped her arms around one of her father's legs and hid her face.

When the soldier reached Papa, he gave a military salute.

Papa acknowledged him with a nod.

"Ensign Carol Jerome Miller with the United States Navy reporting from the U.S. Lighthouse Board in New Orleans, Louisiana. I've just arrived here by boat and I'm looking for…" He reached into his pocket, pulled out some folded paper, and looked at it. "Are you Mr. Jebediah Logan, sir?"

Papa unclasped June from his leg and hoisted her onto his hip. "Yes, I'm Jebediah Logan." He put June on the ground. "Ensign Miller, is it?"

"Yes, sir."

"Has the Union gained control over the Gulf Coast?"

Ensign Miller squinted at Papa. "I can't believe you folks don't even know."

Papa stepped off the porch. "Don't know what?"

"Sir, General Lee surrendered to General Grant at the Appomattox Court House in Virginia back on April the ninth. I'm sorry to be the bearer of bad news, but the war is over and the Confederacy has fallen."

Mama grabbed the porch rail and leaned into it for support. "Do you really mean it? The war is over?"

"Yes, ma'am." Miller's horse nuzzled his ear. He pushed the horse away. "I suppose you don't know that President Lincoln was assassinated either."

Margaret covered her mouth with her hand, horrified. How could the war be over? The war had consumed every hour, every minute, every second of her life for the past four years...and now, just like that, it was over. And President Lincoln...oh, that poor man, and his family. This horrible war had taken so much, so much away from both sides.

"The war is over! The war is over." June began jumping up and down.

Margaret sank into a rocking chair. She was afraid she might drop with all the spinning going on inside her head.

Mama and Papa asked the ensign a myriad of questions.

Margaret's mind was a swirl of unsettling emotions. What had become of Thomas? Did he know the war was over? Was he on his way back for her now?

~*~

Papa invited Ensign Miller inside.

Margaret scraped the last of the ground coffee into the pot. It was barely enough to change the water from clear to brown. She put the pot on the stove and went in to join the others in the front room.

Mama sat next to Papa.

June and Jeremiah sat on the floor, playing with toys. Jeremiah cooed with laughter as June sang her made-up song to him. "The war is over. The war is over. Yippy skippy, yippy skippy, the war is over."

Ensign Miller laughed and then looked at Papa. "Mr. Logan, I was sent here to report that Acting Lighthouse Engineer, M. F. Bonzano, has already prepared a three-story wooden tower in New Orleans to be erected here on Bolivar Point. It has always been common knowledge that the port at Galveston, Texas, is of utmost importance to the United States, and it is imperative that a light be erected as soon as humanly possible."

Papa held Mama's hand, but then let go and scooted to the edge of his seat. "Ensign Miller, I find it hard to believe that the war could be over when only a week ago, a Confederate blockade runner, *The Denbigh*, ran ashore right off the coast here." Papa sounded indignant as he gestured toward the beach. "Most of the crew came ashore after the Union boarded her and set her on fire, for heaven's sake!" Disbelief colored Papa's stark tone.

Miller pulled a pure-white handkerchief from his

pocket and wiped his forehead. "I don't know anything about that, Mr. Logan. I suppose word hasn't trickled down here as yet. I do know that the structure is expected to arrive here sometime in July, and I was sent here to inspect the sight and report back to Engineer Bonzano on my findings." He put his hanky back in his pocket. "Sir, whether you believe the war is over or not, that lighthouse is coming and we need to be ready for it."

"All right, say I believe the war's over and this lighthouse is on its way. What's gonna become of me and my family?"

Ensign Miller put his hands up. "There's no need to be defensive here, Mr. Logan. I didn't come here to cause you or your family any harm. In fact, Engineer Bonzano was quite familiar with the fine work you did at your post back in Louisiana, and I was told that if I found you were still here, to inform you that this post is yours for the taking."

Mama clamped a hand over her mouth and fell back in her chair. She made a strange sound like a cry mixed with glee.

Margaret gasped and clutched her chest.

A rare smile overcame Papa's face and he patted Mama's knee. "That sounds like an interesting offer, Ensign Miller." He looked at Mama and smiled. "But what can you tell me about the New Orleans lights?"

Margaret remembered she had coffee on the stove and rushed to the kitchen. She touched the handle and immediately pulled her hand back. "Ouch." She put two fingers in her mouth and then grabbed a towel for the handle.

"As far as I know, the Port Pontchartrain light was dismantled just as this one was and hasn't been rebuilt, to date. And I believe the New Canal light was relit during the war and the previous keeper is once again manning that station." Miller accepted the cup Margaret handed him. "Thank you, ma'am."

Mama took her cup and then Papa.

"I suppose there's no longer a lighthouse post for us in Louisiana," Papa said.

"Papa, we can't go back to Louisiana. If Elizabeth goes to Austin, we need to stay in Texas. And what if Thomas returns and we're not here? We can't leave, Papa."

Papa raised his hand. "Calm down, Margaret. I know we can't go back, honey." He turned his attention back to Miller and chuckled. "Well, I guess you have your answer, Ensign. We'll take the post."

Miller stood and offered his hand to Papa, who rose and accepted his handshake. "That's wonderful, Mr. Logan. Mr. Bonzano will be pleased to hear the news." He continued to shake Papa's hand. "Oh…and if it's not too much of a burden, I would like to request permission to lodge with you and your family until the erection of the lighthouse is completed."

Papa released his hand and folded his arms. "Well, I suppose that won't be a problem. We're running short on food, but what's one more mouth to feed. We'll find a way."

Miller shook his head. "Oh yes, of course, I almost forgot. I have six months of lighthouse rations with me to give to you and your family. It's back at the dock, waiting to be picked up."

June jumped up from the floor. Her eyes were wide with excitement as she approached Ensign Miller and put her hands on his bent knees. She leaned in. "Is rations food? You brought food for us?"

"Yes, ma'am. I have plenty of food for your whole family."

"Yippee." June twirled around.

Miller patted his breast pocket and pulled out a thick envelope. He handed it to Papa. "This money should cover your expenses."

Papa opened the envelope and thumbed through the bills. A low whistle escaped his lips.

Mama's hand covered her mouth.

Only weeks before, the family worried about how they would pay for Elizabeth's treatment. Now they had more than enough.

Papa leaned toward Mama and put the envelope in her hands. He whispered in her ear, but Margaret overheard what he said. "See, Caroline...didn't I tell you?"

Tears ran down Mama's cheeks. She held the envelope to her chest. "My God will provide. My God will provide."

Margaret offered her own silent prayer of thanksgiving.

29

Margaret hadn't felt so sad since Thomas left with her heart in December. It didn't seem like five months had gone by...it was more like an eternity. Now Elizabeth was leaving too.

Ensign Miller offered the services of his horse to Papa. The dock wasn't far away, but he mentioned that his horse would make the trip in short order so as not to cause Elizabeth too much discomfort. The ensign offered to accompany Papa as far as Galveston because he needed to wire his superiors back in New Orleans on the progress that had been made in preparation for the delivery of the temporary lighthouse.

Papa had mentioned on several occasions how grateful he was to have the young man staying with them. He'd said it was a comfort knowing he would be there should anything happen in his absence.

The whole family was touched by how understanding Miller was about Elizabeth. Even though no one said exactly what was wrong with her, he seemed to comprehend the situation. He assured Papa he would watch after the family in his absence.

Mama didn't utter a word as she loaded some of the rations into a basket for the trip.

"Papa said he would try to buy some fresh fruit for Elizabeth when they get to Galveston."

Mama didn't answer.

"You should have seen June and Jeremiah carrying quilts and pillows out to the cart for Elizabeth to lie on. Those pillows are bigger than they are." She thought surely that would get a reaction from Mama, but she was wrong. "Come on, Mama, let's get this basket outside." Margaret picked up the container of food, linked elbows with Mama, and pulled her out of the kitchen.

Ensign Miller held June and Jeremiah in his arms while they petted his horse on the nose.

Papa loaded Elizabeth's bags into the small cart.

Margaret placed the food basket on top of the other things.

Papa finished loading and then checked the wheels on the cart. "Keep an eye on this wheel when you come back this way. Looks as if there's a loose peg."

Miller put the little ones down and took a look at the wheel. "I will, but don't you worry about it. I'll get you and your daughter to Galveston and on a ferry to the mainland. I suppose you'll be able to catch a stagecoach from there; I don't really know. But you have plenty of money to help you along the way."

Papa nodded at him and turned to Margaret and Mama. "Caroline, I've asked Ensign Miller to help out with some of the heavier chores while I'm gone. Margaret, you know what needs done to keep the place going and you can answer any questions Miller might have."

"Yes, sir."

"June…Jeremiah, do what your mama and Margaret tell you to do, ya hear?"

June put her head down as if he'd given her an

impossible task. "Yes, sir," she answered.

"Is she ready, Margaret?"

"Yes, sir."

Papa went into the house. The screen door slammed shut behind him.

Jeremiah looked at Mama with longing in his eyes. "I go Papa?"

"No, no, Jeremiah. You can't go with Papa. He's taking Elizabeth, not you," June answered.

Mama turned her head away and sobbed silently into a handkerchief. No matter how innocent the words were meant, they worked to pluck out Mama's heart.

"June, why don't you go and open the door for Papa," Margaret said.

June pulled it open just in time for Papa to come through with Elizabeth's thin frame cradled in his arms. Papa laid her in the cart, her head on a pillow. Mama covered her with a quilt and tucked it in around her.

"Mr. Logan, why don't you ride, and I'll walk beside the cart."

"No...I want her to be able to see me. I'll walk."

Miller didn't argue with Papa. He hoisted onto the saddle and patted his horse's neck while the family said their goodbyes.

Papa gestured for them all. "Everyone gather around the wagon. I'd like to say a prayer before we leave. Let's hold hands. Caroline, pick up Elizabeth's hand." He prayed for God to give them safety on the road. He prayed for Mama, Margaret, June, and Jeremiah's safety while he was gone. He spent the most time praying that Elizabeth would be healed. By the time he was finished, they all cried. Tears even rolled down Elizabeth's cheeks.

Margaret lifted Jeremiah over the edge of the cart to say his short goodbye.

Mama held June up to say her long-winded farewell.

Margaret leaned over and kissed Elizabeth on the forehead. "Get well, sister. I love you." She wiped the tears from her face with her apron.

Papa looked at Caroline. "I expect to return before the new lighthouse arrives, but if not, Ensign Miller will be here to carry on with the erection plans without me."

Mama's tears spoke for her.

Papa lifted her chin and kissed her.

Margaret's heart ached watching the love flow between her parents. She wished more than ever that Thomas was there to help them all get through this, but it wasn't to be.

Papa hugged Margaret, June, and Jeremiah and turned to Miller on his horse. "You ready, Ensign?"

"Yes, sir."

Miller flipped the reins up and clicked his tongue. The horse walked down the property line toward the port.

Mama picked up Jeremiah and pulled June close to her side. They waved and hollered goodbye. Mama started sucking in short breaths of air. She set down Jeremiah, put her hand over her mouth, and ran inside the house.

Margaret felt lonelier than the days following Thomas's departure. There was no one to comfort her now...not even Mama, who was so heartbroken she couldn't cope for now.

"I guess it's just us now." She looked down at

June.

"Let's go collect some oysters for supper."

"That sounds like a grand idea. Let's go find the pail."

Margaret did her best to smile, but inside she felt as empty as the deep, dark abyss she saw when she looked into Elizabeth's eyes. Everything was on her shoulders now: the upkeep of the house, her little sister and brother...she even had to watch over Mama. How she longed for Thomas to return. She needed him now more than ever to help her bear this heavy burden. *Oh, Thomas, where could you be? Are you safe and well...alive?*

30

Thomas pulled a grimy neckerchief from his pocket and wiped his brow. The Texas heat was already hotter than any of the places he'd passed through on his long journey back from New York. His thoughts turned to Margaret and her family. How were the Logans faring after the war? Was Margaret still waiting for him? Had she found another love? He prayed every day she hadn't—that she still longed after him as he did for her.

Southern hospitality had become all but nonexistent in the wake of reconstruction and the unwanted influx of Union troops and carpetbaggers. Thomas was fortunate to have his Irish accent and not a northern one. It was a great advantage in helping him land a job.

The long journey landed him in Brenham, Texas, where he found work as a ranch hand. The hard labor and fair wage was welcomed after having worked for practically nothing up north prior to the war. His employer was a good man with Christian values and understood when Thomas told him he would eventually return to south Texas to be with the love of his life.

The sturdy horse pulling the flatbed wagon slowed as Thomas pulled back on the reins. He made the weekly trip into town every Thursday to pick up feed. A man waited on the loading dock for his arrival.

"Good morning, Thomas."

Thomas tipped his head. "Morning, Clayton." He set the reins aside and climbed out of the wagon. "I see ye already have Mr. Giddings's order ready to load."

Clayton pulled on his gloves. "Well, Thomas, you're about as dependable as they come." He hefted one of the bags of feed over his shoulder. "No sense waiting around until you get here."

"That's mighty kind of ye, Clayton. Yer a good man." Thomas pushed back his cowboy hat and scratched his head. "Say, Clayton, would ye mind too much if I were to leave the wagon here while I go make my payment and get a cup of coffee?"

"Naw, you go on ahead. I got this."

"Thank ye kindly, sir."

Thomas crossed the street to Abbi's Diner. His heavy boots kicked up a cloud of dust on the dry road. The bell on the diner door jangled when he opened it. He walked up to the counter and took a seat.

"What'll you have, sir?"

Thomas smiled at the elderly woman. "I've told ye at least a dozen times ye don't have to call me sir. You can call me Thomas, Abbi."

Abbi returned his smile. "Yes, but if I keep doing it, you'll have to correct me and that's about the only way I get to hear that pretty Irish accent of yours." She put her hands on wide hips and chuckled.

"Oh, Abbi, what shall I do with ye? I'll have a cup of coffee, if ye don't mind."

"Coming right up…sir!" The plump little woman turned to get the coffee.

A newspaper, probably left behind from one of

Abbi's breakfast customers, sat on the counter. He looked around to see if anyone was returning for it before picking it up. As he was about to open the paper, a man sitting at the end of the counter caught his attention. He froze in his seat. He blinked a couple times, and then rubbed his eyes to make sure he wasn't imagining things. No, his eyes weren't playing tricks. Thomas got up and put his hand on the man's shoulder.

Mr. Logan dropped his fork into a pool of yellow egg yolks. "Great day in the morning, Thomas Murphy...what on earth are you doing here?"

"Mr. Logan, I can't believe my own eyes." Thomas surrounded him in a great bear hug and firmly patted his back. "What are ye doing way out here?"

"I asked you first, son. What brings you to Brenham, Texas?" Mr. Logan shook his head. "I can't believe I'm really seeing you. Did you make it up to New York? How are your father and brothers doing? Come here, son." Again they shook hands and hugged each other.

"Yes, I did make it to New York. I've so much to tell ye. I wound up here and found that I was in need of a bit more money. I was offered a job at the Giddings Ranch just east of town and I took it."

Abbi stood across the counter from the two men, coffee in hand. "Am I to assume you'll be taking your coffee down here now?" The plump little woman laughed out of habit.

"Oh yes, Abbi, this is Mr. Logan, Margaret's papa."

She set the coffee on the counter and her eyes got wide. "Well, I'll be. I've heard so much about your family...especially that Margaret of yours. From what I hear, she's quite the girl."

Mr. Logan grinned at her. "Thank you, ma'am. We're real proud of all our children."

"Well, of course you are. I'm going to let you two get back to talking. Give me a holler if y'all need anything."

"Thank ye, Abbi," Thomas said. He turned his attention back to Mr. Logan. "All right, now ye know why I'm here. Tell me what you're doing here."

"I'm on my way back home from taking Elizabeth to the state hospital in Austin." Mr. Logan closed his eyes and when he opened them, tears glistened before he blinked them away.

"Oh no, what happened? Is she going to be all right?"

Mr. Logan rested his elbow on the counter and shook his head. "It's...it's a hospital for people that have sickness in their head. We didn't know what else to do with her."

"Oh, I'm so sorry, sir. Do they think they can help her?"

"I don't know, son. I talked with the superintendent, and he said there was a good chance they could." He looked away. "I sure hope so."

Thomas hurt for him. The man loved his children. He put his hand on Mr. Logan's shoulder. "I'm sure they will do their best, sir."

"I pray you're right, son." Mr. Logan turned back to his plate and picked up a slice of toast. "So tell me about your trip up north."

Thomas folded his arms on the counter and then looked at his reflection in the big framed mirror on the back wall. "It was a fine trip. My father is doing well and my youngest brother, Michael, is too. But actually, they're not even in New York anymore."

"Oh, really? Why is that?"

"Well, it seems Michael turned out to be quite gifted in the field of medicine and was sent up to Massachusetts General Hospital to train with the experts there."

"Well, how about that. Good for him. So I guess they're doing just fine for themselves."

"I suppose so, but I'm afraid there was some bad news. My other brother, Jonathan, is among the missing."

"Oh no, Thomas, I'm so sorry to hear that." Mr. Logan's face was sorrowful.

"Aye, but for the grace of God and the kindness of the Logan family, I would be dead too."

The older man patted Thomas on the shoulder. "But God had a bigger plan for your life, son. He sent you all the way to Bolivar, Texas, just so you could marry my daughter Margaret."

Thomas felt his heart leap at the mention of her name. "Oh, Mr. Logan, please tell me she's still waiting for me. I never even got the chance to ask for her hand."

Mr. Logan smiled and took a bite of his toast. "Of course she's waiting for you, Thomas. And why wouldn't she be? That girl is in love with you."

Thomas looked up and released a long huff of air. "Thank Ye, Lord. Ye answered my prayers."

Mr. Logan chuckled at his reaction. "So tell me, son, I thought you were collecting your Navy wages to get back to the peninsula. Why are you here, working on a ranch?"

Thomas felt the heat rising up his neck. "I did receive my pay, but a good bit of it went toward my fare back here. And I didn't want to return to Margaret empty-handed." He rubbed at the war wound on his head. "I've still got a good amount of my war wages, but I've been working here to pay for the wedding ring I bought her."

"Well, look at you." Mr. Logan grinned. "If I didn't know any better, I'd think you were trying to impress my little girl."

Thomas returned the smile. "Aye, that I am, sir."

Mr. Logan put some cash on the counter and stood. "Well, come on, son, I want to see this ring."

"But it's not paid for yet. It's still at the mercantile."

"How much do you still owe on it?"

"Three payments is all." A look of satisfaction graced Thomas's face. "I've set aside money to start on a house for the two of us as well."

"That's wonderful. Can we go take a look at this ring you've purchased?"

"Sure, I'm on my way there now to make a payment." Thomas picked up his coffee and took a sip...cold. He didn't need it anyway. The visit with Mr. Logan was more exciting than any cup of coffee.

They said their goodbyes to Abbi and left the diner with the doorbell jingling in their wake. A few blocks down, they entered Feinberg's Emporium.

"Thomas, I've been wondering what happened to you." Mr. Feinberg pushed his hat back on his head, revealing the small amount of hair he had left.

"Aye, sir, I was on my way over when I ran into Mr. Logan, Margaret's papa."

Feinberg's eyes grew wide. He grabbed Mr. Logan's hand and gave it a forceful shake. "It's so nice to meet you, Mr. Logan. Thomas here has told me so much about your daughter."

"Nice to meet you too, sir." Mr. Logan looked a bit startled at the reception.

The frail little man brought a file box out from beneath the counter and thumbed through it. "Murphy, Murphy, let's see. Ah, here it is." He pulled out an envelope with a receipt pasted to the front and Thomas's ring inside. "Just three more payments and she's all yours. Isn't that exciting?"

Thomas put his hand in his pocket to pull out his money. Before he could count out enough for the payment, Mr. Logan slapped a stack of cash down on top of the receipt.

Thomas looked at him. "Wh-what are you doing, sir?"

"There…paid in full." Mr. Logan looked at him. "Now there's nothing keeping you here."

"I don't believe it."

Feinberg threw back his head and laughed. "Believe it, Thomas. You have yourself a very good future father-in-law!" Feinberg took the ring out of the envelope and slipped it on his pinky. He stamped the envelope *paid* in big red letters and then disappeared under the counter. When he stood up, he held a little gold box. He placed the ring inside and handed it to Thomas. "There you go, Thomas. Now go ask Miss Margaret to marry you."

Thomas was still in shock when they left the mercantile. His mind raced with questions concerning what he should do next. Then he remembered the main reason he was in town. He glanced over toward the feed store.

Mr. Logan interrupted his thoughts. "Well, Thomas, can I talk you into returning to Bolivar with me? Stage leaves at two."

He didn't know where to start. "I...yes...but I have to deliver the feed. But we don't need to take the stage...I have my own horse and wagon now." Thomas started laughing. It was the first time he'd laughed in a very long time. He handed Margaret's ring to Mr. Logan. "Thank ye so much for everything, sir."

Mr. Logan took a long look at the ring. "Mighty fine-looking ring, son." He returned the box to Thomas. "Well, all right then. Let's deliver that feed and go tell your boss you've got yourself a better offer." He put his arm around Thomas's shoulder and they walked together to fetch the wagon.

Thomas's thoughts fled to a small peninsula in the Gulf of Mexico where the love of his life resided. He longed to look into her violet eyes...to smell her raven hair...to kiss her ruby lips. And now, thanks to her papa, he would have her in his arms sooner than he'd expected. And sooner was a very good thing.

31

Margaret pulled the last little pair of overalls from the washtub and twisted them round and round, allowing the water to flow back into the tub. When the pants stopped dripping, she tossed the twisted ball into the basket on the floor beside her. She looked at her hands, red and aching from the soap, the scrubbing, and the twisting. And worst of all, the clothes weren't even finished. They still had to be hung on the line to dry.

Mama came in the kitchen and dumped another load of laundry into the washtub. Margaret let her head drop back. "Ugh, Mama, how dare you?" she half-teased and held her hands up for Mama to see. "Look at my hands. They look like little lobster claws."

"I'm sorry, honey, but until they invent some fancy machine that does the washing for us, I'm afraid this is our lot in life." Mama stirred the pot of soup cooking on the stove.

"Soup smells good." Margaret pushed the new pile of clothes down into the water to soak. "You sure made a big pot of it."

"Thank you. I don't know how to make this recipe any smaller. Sure wish your papa was here to enjoy it. It's his favorite."

Margaret sat down at the kitchen table and wiped

her hands on a towel. "Wonder how Papa is faring and if Elizabeth is doing well at the asylum."

Mama poured a cup of coffee and sat down. "I've been wondering that myself. Seems as if they've been gone an awful long time, but I don't know how far it is to Austin…could take a long time, for all I know."

Mama missed Papa and Elizabeth. Sadness continued to follow her through the days. Not even Jeremiah's chubby cheeks made her smile.

"I sure hope Papa was right about them being able to help Elizabeth." Margaret missed her sister too. But her loss was tempered with the fact that Elizabeth had disappeared into herself long before she left for the asylum. "I've never seen anyone in such a bad way…well, except for Mr. Langley's son, that is." Margaret swirled her finger around on the tablecloth, intentionally not making eye contact with Mama.

"Yes, his passing was so sad, but in some ways it was a blessing. Sometimes when people are so bad off, it seems better if God just goes on and takes them home." Mama stirred a spoonful of honey into her coffee. "Poor boy, his brain was so far gone he didn't even know who his papa was anymore."

Margaret looked at her blotchy red hands and her broken fingernails. "He sure didn't last long when he took the fever."

"No, he sure didn't." She took a sip of coffee.

"It was good of you and Papa to minister to Mr. Langley after he passed."

"Well, it was the Christian thing to do. And because we did, we made a new friend." Mama held the cup of coffee between two hands as she spoke. "Mr. Langley really did care about Elizabeth, you know. He told us that many a time when we took food over to him."

"I know, Mama. We all care very much about Elizabeth." Margaret returned to the washtub. "I just pray she gets the help she needs."

"I do too, honey."

Margaret plunged back into the washing and dreamed of Thomas. She silently prayed for his safety…wherever he was.

Mama tended to the boiling pot of soup.

"Oh, Mama, wouldn't it be lovely if I was washing clothes for Thomas and my very own family?"

Mama shook her head. "Margaret, it wouldn't matter if you were doing the wash for Queen Victoria, believe me, it wouldn't be lovely."

Did Mama actually make a joke? Margaret pulled her hands out of the tub and flicked water at her.

Mama's eyes grew wide.

Margaret started laughing…then Mama laughed too. Margaret went to her mother and put her arms around her. She thanked God for the laughter even though she knew it was only a mask to hide Mama's sadness.

The front screen door opened and slammed shut.

"Mama, Mama!" June rushed into the kitchen and nearly ran over Margaret and Mama. She looked at the two of them hugging each other. "OK…" She then seemed to remember what she came in for and shouted as loud as she had when she first came in. "Mama?"

Margaret released Mama.

"What is it, June?" Mama asked.

"Mama, Papa's coming up the road in an honest-to-goodness horse and buggy. And…and he ain't alone." June turned around and ran back out of the house.

Mama folded her hands and looked heavenward. "Thank You, Jesus." As she said the words, tears started to fall.

~*~

Thomas flipped the reins. "Come on, Fargus, get, get." The closer he came to Margaret, the more he hastened the horse.

Mr. Logan held onto his hat. "Take it easy, son. We want to get there in one piece."

"I'm sorry, sir, but we're almost there, and I'm wanting to see yer daughter something awful."

Mr. Logan laughed at him. "Yep, there's someone there I'm wanting to see something awful too, son."

June ran out the front door with Mrs. Logan close behind.

Jeremiah toddled after them, running on sturdy little legs.

A man came from around the house. Must be the Navy man Mr. Logan had told him about. But where was Margaret?

Mr. Logan hopped off the wagon when Thomas eased Fargus to a stop.

"Papa, Papa, you're home." June jumped into Papa's outstretched arms.

Mrs. Logan noticed him and her eyes lit up even more.

Mr. Logan put June on the ground and swung Jeremiah in the air. The baby chortled with glee. Mr. Logan set him back on the ground.

Mr. and Mrs. Logan hugged and kissed.

June ran to Thomas and held her hands up, wanting him to pick her up.

"Where's Margaret, young'un?"

June giggled, put her hands on his cheeks, and shook his face. "She don't know you're here, silly."

Thomas turned toward the house when the screen door opened.

Margaret stepped onto the porch. She smiled at the sight of her parents' joyous reunion. And then her gaze met his. Her hand flew to her mouth. She stepped off the porch and ran to him.

He put June on the ground and rushed to meet her halfway. When they reached each other, Margaret fell into his embrace. She didn't even look at his face. She held him tight, and he had no objection to it. Thomas lifted her chin and kissed her with the passion of having been apart for six long months.

Everything came to a complete stop while they held each other. The rest of the world faded away and it was as if they were the last two people left on earth.

"Ewwww." June scowled at them and her nose scrunched up.

Margaret looked up at him, her cheeks a bold red. A smile crept onto her face.

Thomas let out a small chuckle, and then they both laughed...loud and long.

Mrs. Logan stepped away from Mr. Logan long enough to give Thomas a big hug. "Well, isn't this a surprise? How in the world did Jeb find you?"

Thomas released Margaret's hand and she hugged her papa. "It's hard to believe, ma'am, but yer husband and I ran into each other in Brenham, Texas."

"Brenham, Texas," Mrs. Logan repeated.

"Yes, ma'am....Texas is a mighty big state, but it certainly is a small world."

Mrs. Logan gasped. "Oh, my goodness, I was so

shocked at seeing the both of you together that I forgot to ask about Elizabeth!"

Mr. Logan raised his hand. "She's just fine, Caroline. They're giving her the best treatment available, and I was told we would receive an update very soon." He gestured to Ensign Miller. "Thomas, I want you to meet Ensign Carol Jerome Miller."

Thomas held his hand out. "Nice to meet ye, Ensign Miller."

"Nice to meet you, Thomas, but you can call me Jerry."

"Well, Jerry, Mr. Logan tells me you've been taking care of his fine family in his absence."

"Yes, but it's been the other way around. They've taken good care of me." He patted his belly. "Couple of fine cooks you have here."

Mr. Logan smiled and nodded his head. "That's for sure." He released Margaret's hand, put his arm around his wife's shoulders, and squeezed her tight. "Can't wait to eat some of Mama's good grub."

Mrs. Logan smiled and nestled close to his side.

"Mr. Logan, I've received word that the tower is scheduled to ship out of New Orleans in early July. I've spent the past few weeks clearing off the pad sight, but there's still a lot of work to be done before its arrival."

"Yep, plenty of foliage has taken over the pad in the past three years or more."

"Yes, sir," Jerry said before he turned to Thomas. "Margaret here tells me you're a Navy man like myself."

"Yes, that I am."

"Well, I was wondering if you might be interested in a job. You can help me finish clearing the sight and as soon as the tower arrives, you can assist in the erection."

"I'd very much like that...Jerry." Thomas felt strange calling a junior naval officer by his first name. "I'd like to talk to you about that, but first, there's something I've waited a very long time to do." Thomas took Margaret's hands into his. He knelt down before her. "I know this isn't very romantic, but here goes. Margaret Frances Logan, I've loved ye since the first time I set eyes on ye that day on the beach. I thought ye were an angel come to take me up to heaven. But instead, ye saved my life. We've been through some good times, and we've been through some bad times, and through it all I've loved ye with all my heart. So I ask ye today, Margaret Logan...will ye do me the honor of marrying me, lass?" Thomas looked into her eyes, trying to judge the outcome. He wasn't sure if the look on Margaret's face meant she would laugh or cry until she fell to her knees and threw her arms around him.

"Oh, yes, yes, of course I'll marry you, Thomas Murphy!"

32

Margaret's shoulders dropped as the long sigh slipped out and she wiped her brow. "Oh, my goodness, it's hot!" She waved a hand, fanning herself. "You know, Mama, I'll bet if you put all the purple hull peas we've shelled together into one big pot, it would be so big we wouldn't be able to fit it into the kitchen."

"Oh, I don't know about all that, but we have shelled many a pea in our days. Sometimes peas were all we had to live on, and I was sure glad to have them." Mama didn't look up from her work. "Don't throw out those pods. Put them in that sack I brought out. I thought we would try that pig of yours on them."

A warm breeze floated in from the coast. It wasn't refreshing, but it gave a hint of relief to the blazing August heat. Margaret wasn't paying a bit of attention to what Mama said. Her eyes were firmly planted on her handsome husband-to-be.

He worked with his shirt off; his muscular arms glistened with sweat.

The blush creeping up her neck and cheeks wasn't only caused by the heat of the day.

Thomas, Papa, and Ensign Miller worked together with the crew from New Orleans to unload the wooden tower that would become the temporary lighthouse. The Union was anxious to relight the waterway between the Bolivar Peninsula and Texas's largest city, Galveston.

Margaret heard her piglet squeal in distress.

June was chasing her baby around, holding on to the pig's tail. Jeremiah followed close behind, holding on to her skirt.

"Hey, you two, let him be. You're wearing out my present from Thomas."

June released the baby pig, then she and Jeremiah fell to the ground in a laughing heap.

"I don't know how you put up with those two, Mama."

"I had plenty of practice putting up with you and your sister."

"I suppose so."

Margaret glanced down at the bowl of peas and straightened the skirt of her simple blue work dress bunched up around the container. She realized something in that moment. For the first time since her family had moved to Texas, she felt contented. The burning desire in the back of her mind to return to New Orleans wasn't there. She couldn't remember the last time she'd thought about wanting to wear fancy ball gowns or attend social parties. That part of her life had passed away with the war. It all seemed like vanity to her now.

She was happy just the way she was. And she no longer thought of Bolivar as a godforsaken place. She was happy to make Texas her new home. Yes, Texas had grown on all of them. It would be the new home for the Logan family and soon the Murphy family as well.

Her eyes drifted to the east, to where Thomas had begun setting the piers of what would be the foundation of their home. Thomas had purchased the small piece of land. Their hopes and dreams of a life filled with love and someday a family would become a reality on that tiny slice of heaven.

Mama was still shelling her bowl of peas.

"Can you believe what a coincidence it was that Papa and Thomas met up in Brenham and how things have worked out so perfectly? Just think about it. The war is over, and both Thomas and Papa have jobs, and—"

"Now you wait just one minute, Margaret Frances Logan. You know good and well that none of those things were coincidences. God was in control of every single thing that happened. Now are you shelling those peas, or will I have to do it for you?"

Mama's words hit Margaret like a load of bricks. God *was* in control or else she never would have fallen in love with Thomas. The hatred she once held in her heart for northerners had faded into the past and she was pledged to wed a Yankee. She'd forgotten all about the money from the Lighthouse Board that arrived right when they needed it to get help for Elizabeth. No, there were no coincidences…only divine assistance. She turned toward her mama. "How did you get to be so smart, Mama?"

"I serve a gracious God, who gives wisdom to those who need it." She chuckled. "And the good Lord knows I've needed it."

"Have you and Papa thought any more about the wedding? Did y'all ever decide whether we're going to have it inside or outside?"

"Oh, for heaven's sake, of course we've thought about it, but no, we haven't made any firm decisions yet. That's the least of our worries. We have to think about how many of the neighbors might come out for the wedding and how much food we'll need. Goodness, the list goes on and on." She turned to Margaret and smiled. "You should be more concerned about me finishing the alterations on your dress before the day of the wedding."

Margaret sighed. "Yes, ma'am. I'm just so excited and it will be here before you know it."

"I'm aware of that and it will get taken care of. But not if you don't help me out by shelling those peas. Good thing I know how to cook for a small army."

There were so many things that needed done, but her biggest worry—how to get Elizabeth back home from Austin for the wedding. She rustled her fingers in the bowl of pea pods. "I saw that Papa received a letter from the hospital. Did they decide whether or not Elizabeth can come home for the wedding?"

Mama gave "the look." "Nosiness doesn't suit you, dear."

"At least I didn't open it." Margaret grinned.

"Be thankful you didn't, young lady." Mama nodded toward her bowl, implying she should actually shell the peas instead of simply stirring them about. "And if it is any of your business, Dr. Walker is completely against Elizabeth leaving the hospital after such a short period of time. They've only just started making progress in her treatment."

"But she's got to be at my wedding, Mama. I can't get married without my sister standing by my side."

"Don't you think I want her to be here with us just as much as you do? Now what do you think is more important…Elizabeth coming home for your wedding, or her staying at the hospital and getting well?"

"You know the answer to that, Mama, but I've had

my wedding planned out ever since Jeremiah was born. He would be my little pageboy, and June would be my flower girl." Her voice began to crack as her throat tightened. "And...and Elizabeth would stand with me at the altar. Besides, we can take her back to the hospital just as soon as the wedding is over."

"I'm sorry, honey, but I don't want you to get your hopes up. Things don't always turn out the way we dream they will."

Margaret returned to shelling peas. Her disappointment that there were so many things over which she had no control angered her to the bone. She couldn't put off the wedding until Elizabeth was well...who knew how long that might be?

Thomas was getting more anxious by the day to have her as his wife.

She would have to put away the wedding she had always dreamed of and settle for what God would allow her. As the number of hulled peas in her bowl grew, so did the mountain of grief in her heart. There had to be some way for Elizabeth to come to the wedding, but how? *Lord, I don't pretend to think I'm in control of anything down here. I acknowledge Your Lordship and give this whole wedding over to You. And if it's in Your will that Elizabeth be at my wedding, then You'll have to make it happen. Please forgive me for my lack of faith. In Your Son's name I pray.*

It was a relief to give everything up to God. Now she could concentrate on more important things...like watching her husband-to-be working without his shirt on.

33

Have not I commanded thee? Be strong and of a good courage. For the Lord thy God is with thee whithersoever thou goest. Thomas repeated the verse in his mind, but it did little to ease his rattled nerves. He could hardly believe it had only been a year and one month since he'd first laid eyes on Margaret and now he stood at the altar ready to marry her.

His brand-new suit had arrived just in time for the wedding. Everything had worked out, including the arrival of Bolivar's newest resident, the Reverend Phillip Everly, all the way from Tuscaloosa, Alabama.

Mrs. Everly sat on the second row, looking more in control than any woman Thomas had ever encountered. Her five little charges sat beside her, from youngest to oldest, with legs crossed and backs straight. Thomas doubted they were such angels when their mother had her back turned.

Mrs. Logan sat up front. She dabbed at her eye with a fancy hanky. Thomas had never seen it before and figured she'd had it put away for an important event such as her daughter's wedding.

He managed a weak smile in her direction. It was the best he could do with the antics going on inside his stomach. A pang of grief washed over him that his own mother couldn't be there to witness his marriage.

Reverend Everly made a gesture and the high-pitched whine of a violin chord cut through the cool autumn air. Mr. Langley sat with the instrument wedged beneath his chin. A hushed silence came over the small crowd gathered there.

So much change had come to pass with the end of the war. No one would have believed this man, who had only months earlier threatened to turn Thomas in to the Confederates, was now a good friend of the Logans. So much so that he was willing to provide the music at the wedding. There truly was no limit to what God could do in the lives and hearts of His children.

Thomas nearly jumped out of his skin when a hand clamped around his shoulder. He took a deep breath and wiped the beads of sweat from his upper lip. "What are ye trying to do, Miller...scare the life out of me?"

Ensign Miller chuckled and patted Thomas's shoulder. "Get a grip on yourself, man. It's your wedding day. Try to enjoy it."

"Aye, yer right." Thomas shrugged his shoulders. "I'm just a bit jumpy." Thomas adjusted his suit coat and shook his arms.

Miller and Thomas had become fast friends over the past few months of working together. And since his own brother couldn't make it to Texas for the wedding, he was happy to have a friend standing by his side for support. It was a comfort knowing he would be taking Margaret to meet his brother and father soon after they were married.

~*~

Margaret knelt down to Jeremiah's eye level and

put her hands around his small arms. "All right now, Jeremiah, you know what to do, right?" Just to make sure, she gave a quick reminder of his duties. "You walk down between all those people sitting in chairs out there, OK?"

He shook his head and frowned.

Margaret scratched at a bit of food on his cheek, only making his frown deepen. She softened her voice and smiled at her little brother. "But you're all dressed up in your best pair of overalls, and you get to carry this pretty pillow Mama made!" She showed him the small pink pillow Mama had adorned with ribbons. "Feel how soft it is." He rubbed the fabric with his tiny hand. "Will you do it for sissy?" The extra syrup in her voice must have done the trick, as Jeremiah closed his eyes and nodded his head. Margaret put the pillow in his hands and turned him toward the sheet they used as a curtain to hide behind. "Good boy. Now walk down to where Thomas is." She patted him on the bottom and sent him on his way.

From the sounds coming from those in attendance, it was clear they liked her idea of having Jeremiah walk as a pageboy in the ceremony.

Papa had missed the whole exchange between the two of them, as he was occupied retying all the loose ribbons June had undone on her dress while they waited for the wedding to begin. Margaret peeked around the sheet to see Jeremiah run down the aisle before jumping into Mama's lap. She shook her head and smiled.

"Margaret, get over here and help me get June's clothes back on her!"

"Yes, Papa." She finished tying the ribbons Papa had missed and admired how beautiful her little sister looked. Mama had saved back the pale blue dress that had been passed down from one sister to the next. Now it was June's turn to wear it on this special day. Margaret wanted to cry tears of joy. "Oh, June Marie, you look so pretty."

June threw her arms around Margaret's waist and squeezed her tight. "So do you, sissy." She then gasped and slapped her hands onto her cheeks. "Where's my flower-girl basket?"

"I got it right here." Papa handed it to her.

"Whew, that was close." She took the basket from Papa and headed out from behind the sheet, making her presence known. "Here comes the flower girl."

Laughter filled the air as June walked down between the two rows of chairs. She threw the flower heads on the ground like a little princess. All was fine and good until she came to the reverend's family and took a whole handful of the dried flowers and, for some unknown reason, flung them at Reverend Everly's middle boy.

Margaret looked heavenward and shook her head.

Mama jumped from her chair and snatched June from the aisle.

Margaret turned back to Papa and tears welled up in her eyes. He hugged Elizabeth and pressed her head against his shoulder. Even though the doctors weren't in favor of her coming home, the final decision was Papa's to make and he had allowed it.

Margaret couldn't believe how far Papa was willing to go to make her wedding perfect. And he had succeeded.

Elizabeth wore one of Margaret's prettier hand-me-down dresses. Mama had to take in the seams to fit her now-tiny frame.

Papa released Elizabeth and gestured toward Margaret, who was holding her hands out to her. Even though Elizabeth had gained back some of her lost weight, Margaret felt her rib bones as they embraced. It was hard for Margaret not to cry, especially seeing Papa with tears in his eyes.

"I'm so happy you could be here for the wedding."

Elizabeth held her at arm's length and smiled. She lifted her hand to Margaret's face and wiped away a tear. "I'm happy to be here too." She hugged her sister again. "And I'm happy that you are marrying Thomas. I...I almost ruined everything."

Margaret patted her back. "Oh, hush up. You didn't ruin a thing. Everything turned out perfect. Now get out there before Mr. Langley's arm falls off from playing that violin for too long."

Elizabeth smiled as Papa pulled the sheet back for her. He kissed her on the cheek and handed her a small bouquet of wildflowers tied together with a satin ribbon. She turned and winked at Margaret before heading toward Thomas and the minister.

Margaret picked up the last accessory left on the porch swing, her own bouquet of wildflowers. She ran her fingers down the length of the blue satin ribbon before looking into Papa's eyes.

He cupped his palms around her face. "You know how proud I am of you?"

"What do you mean, Papa?"

"Honey, I don't know of any young woman who could have made it through all you have and still have so much love in your heart and a beautiful smile on your face."

She hugged him tight. "Oh, Papa, it's not me at all.

I give God all the credit...and you and Mama, of course." She didn't want to cry on her wedding day, but it was too late. She wiped her eyes and tried to put a big smile on her face. "All right now, there are people waiting for us."

Papa lowered the veil over her face and offered his arm to her as they hooked elbows.

The sheet was pulled back a final time, allowing everyone in attendance to see the bride.

She didn't see anyone but the love of her life, Thomas Murphy.

~*~

The makeshift curtain had opened and closed so many times Thomas wasn't sure if Margaret was ever coming out, but this time, he saw her. Mr. Langley must have stopped playing his violin because he no longer heard the music.

Everyone in attendance turned toward the curtain and stood as she and her papa appeared.

Thomas had never seen her look so majestically beautiful as when she walked down the aisle. The nervousness he'd felt earlier seemed to have melted out through his legs, leaving them mushy as fresh butter in August.

Even though the gown had belonged to Mrs. Logan, it appeared to have been made especially for his bride-to-be. The soft peach-colored fabric made her skin appear darker than usual.

Thomas peered at her bare shoulders for the first time and it took his breath away. Raven hair peeked out beneath the veil covering her face. He could make out the color of her violet eyes, sparkling behind her veil. Never had he seen a more beautiful woman in his life, and she was about to become his…forever.

Mr. Logan paused before reaching him and pulled the veil back, revealing Margaret's face.

Thomas sucked in a deep breath and let it out slowly.

Mrs. Logan sniffed and put the hanky up to her nose when Mr. Logan kissed his daughter on the cheek and put her hand in Thomas's. He then sat down next to his wife and held her hand.

Margaret took her place next to Thomas. She held his hand and looked into his eyes, melting away any fears he held.

Reverend Everly cleared his throat, and they both smiled and turned toward him.

"Thomas and Margaret have asked that I read these passages found in the book of Ruth. The truths held here in these verses will forever be a holy pledge between Thomas Murphy and Margaret Logan.

"And Ruth said, Intreat me not to leave thee, or to return from following after thee: for whither thou goest, I will go; and where thou lodgest, I will lodge: thy people shall be my people, and thy God my God. Where thou diest, will I die, and there will I be buried: the Lord do so to me, and more also, if ought but death part thee and me." The reverend closed his Bible. "Please bow your heads."

Everyone bowed their heads as Reverend Everly prayed.

Except Thomas and Margaret. While words were being sent to God on their behalf, the young couple gazed into each other's eyes. No words were spoken, but in those few brief moments an unspeakable amount of love passed between them.

Thomas repeated the vows as instructed by the

reverend. "I, Thomas Murphy, take thee, Margaret Logan, to be my wedded wife, to have and to hold from this day forward, for better, for worse, for richer, for poorer, in sickness and in health, to love and to cherish, till death us do part."

It was at that moment when Margaret began to say her vows that Thomas realized the wonderful thing that was about to happen. When Margaret said those two little words...*I do*...their lives would forever be entwined together. He would be her husband, and she would be his wife, and the two would become one flesh.

34

Margaret hadn't seen so much food since before the war began. The neighbors had been more than generous in sharing what they had to make the wedding feast a success. They hadn't forgotten Papa and Mama's generosity with the lighthouse rations.

Flour and sugar were available again, although in short supply, allowing them to have a whole table devoted to sweets. The fruit pies, cookies, and cakes made that particular table the most popular of them all, especially with June, Jeremiah, and the Everly children.

Mama looked happier than ever, sitting at one of the tables, talking with all the neighbor ladies, both new and old. Now that word the war was over spread through the South, it wasn't unusual for families to come outside and visit with each other. Little by little, people found they didn't have to look over their shoulders at every noise. Slowly but surely, the fear of being shot, raided, or captured became a distant memory.

Things weren't as they were before the war...and they never would be again.

Margaret remembered with great pleasure the day Necie came running up to the house, busting to tell her good news. She was leaving Bolivar and going back to Louisiana to find her Moses. Margaret glowed with pride for her friend. Yes, things would never be the same again, and for that, Margaret couldn't have been more thankful.

There were so many people to meet and greet following the wedding that Margaret was glad to finally sit down at the table next to Mama. It delighted her to see Mama talking and laughing with the new friends she had made. Mama would need their friendship and support once she and Thomas left for Massachusetts.

Margaret took a deep breath and touched the collar of her dress. She felt red blotches rising on her neck at the very thought of their honeymoon. *Oh, Father, tonight is the night. I'm so scared and excited at the same time. What did Mama mean when she said all my fears would be gone with the morning?* Margaret smiled at an embarrassing thought and forced her mind in a different direction.

She would soon meet Thomas's father and brother. It just occurred to her that she now had a father-in-law and a brother-in-law. Just thinking about traveling across the country made her giddy with excitement. Margaret snuggled against Mama's arm. She didn't feel like a married woman. She still felt like the oldest daughter of Jebediah and Caroline Logan; big sister to Elizabeth, June, and Jeremiah. One glance down at her ring finger told her otherwise. She was now Mrs. Margaret Frances Murphy, wife of Thomas Murphy. She liked how it sounded even if the idea of being a wife scared her a bit.

It thrilled Margaret's soul to see Elizabeth talking and laughing with Mr. Langley. He truly seemed to love her as one of his own. She'd been a great help to him with his son Tommy. Her heart was in the right place even if her mind had betrayed her. But Elizabeth had come a long way in her treatment, and hopefully, she would be cured soon. Anything was better than the miserable state she had been in before they took her to the hospital. That was a comfort to Margaret, indeed, to their whole family.

Her papa, Ensign Miller, and some of the other neighbor men were talking away. The locals had accepted Thomas into the fold. Only months before, these same neighbors would have been willing to string her husband up, but now he fit right in as though he was one of them.

Mr. Langley put his violin in position and played a toe-tapping jig.

Four little icing-faced children were coaxed out from under the dessert table by the upbeat rhythm—of course, June and Jeremiah were two of the four.

Elizabeth clapped her hands in time to the music as she walked toward the table where Margaret, Mama, and the other ladies sat.

Margaret nudged Mama. "Would you just look at your children? They've eaten almost all the sweets and now they're covered with icing and dirt. They're leading Reverend Everly's children down the wayward path, Mama."

One of the elderly ladies waved her hand at Margaret. "Oh, just let them have their fun, honey. It's not every day we have a wedding here on the peninsula."

The ladies all laughed and carried on with their chatter.

Elizabeth sat down next to Margaret and hugged

her arm. "They are having fun," Elizabeth said. "Look at them dancing and spinning around as if they don't have a care in the world."

Margaret pointed at Jeremiah. "Yes, indeed, look at our baby brother. I believe he's eaten too many sweets." They laughed aloud when he spun himself to dizziness and fell on his bottom. "Mama, you might as well start drawing up some bath water now. Jeremiah will need a soak in the washtub tonight."

Elizabeth held tight to Margaret's arm. "I'm so glad you wanted me to be here for your wedding. I wouldn't have wanted to miss all this."

Margaret pressed Elizabeth's head against her shoulder. It felt wonderful having her sister back. "I wouldn't have it any other way." A thought crossed Margaret's mind. "You know, sister…you don't have to go back to the hospital when Thomas and I leave for Massachusetts. You can tell Mama and Papa you want to stay here."

Elizabeth released a long sigh. "I know." She patted Margaret's arm. "But I really want to go back."

"Why? Wouldn't you rather stay here with family? You're so much better now."

"I know it's hard for you to understand, but it's better for me there. Most everyone there is like…me." Elizabeth's eyes brightened at whatever she was thinking about. "Margaret, it's such a beautiful place. There's a huge garden and the most magnificent trees you've ever seen. Oh, and I have my duties to attend to. Did Mama tell you I'm teaching Bible lessons to the young women who want to learn?"

Margaret was dumbfounded. "No, I had no idea. I thought you would want to stay here. I never thought about you wanting to go back there."

Elizabeth smiled. "And there's something else too."

"Oh…what is it?"

Elizabeth blushed. "There's a boy there that I like."

Margaret's eyes grew wide. "Elizabeth Fay…you have a boyfriend."

The sisters giggled like they were little girls again and fell into each other's arms. The laughter was healing and apparently contagious, as the others ladies gathered at the table began chuckling too.

Thomas made his way toward the gaggle of giggling women. He acknowledged Elizabeth with a tip of his hat. "Ma'am." He offered his hand to Margaret. "May I have this dance, Mrs. Murphy?"

"Why, of course, Mr. Murphy." She accepted his outstretched hand and rose to her feet. "Would you please excuse me, Elizabeth?"

"Yes, of course."

Margaret allowed her husband to pull her out amongst the band of dancing, twirling children. Thomas bowed to her and she returned with a curtsy. He held his hand out to her. "May I?"

She paused as an impish grin crept across her face. "I don't know, sir…does this mean you will love me forever?"

Thomas smiled back at her. "M'lady, I shall love you forever and a day."

"All right then, yes, you may."

She took his hand and they joined together in dancing a reel. As Thomas spun her around, she couldn't help but think how much the dance reminded her of their whirlwind romance. And even though things got off to a rough start, she knew in her heart that God had orchestrated every movement of the dance. He had set the wheels in motion to make her the happiest woman on earth.

As the music played faster and faster, Margaret held on tight to the arms of the dance partner she would cherish for the rest of her life.

Thank you

We appreciate you reading this White Rose Publishing title. For other inspirational stories, please visit our online bookstore at www.pelicanbookgroup.com.

For questions or more information, contact us at customer@pelicanbookgroup.com.

White Rose Publishing
Where Faith is the Cornerstone of Love™
an imprint of Pelican Ventures Book Group
www.PelicanBookGroup.com

Connect with Us
www.facebook.com/Pelicanbookgroup
www.twitter.com/pelicanbookgrp

To receive news and specials, subscribe to our bulletin
http://pelink.us/bulletin

May God's glory shine through
this inspirational work of fiction.

AMDG

Free Book Offer

We're looking for booklovers like you to partner with us! Join our team of influencers today and receive at least one free eBook per month. Maybe more!

For more information
Visit http://pelicanbookgroup.com/booklovers
or e-mail
booklovers@pelicanbookgroup.com